RESISTANCE TO MAGIC

RESISTANCE TO MAGIC

THE SARIAH CHRONICLES™ BOOK ONE

PETER GLENN

MICHAEL ANDERLE

LMBPN

DISRUPTIVE IMAGINATION

Copyright © LMBPN Publishing
Cover by Mihaela Voicu http://www.mihaelavoicu.com/
Cover copyright © LMBPN Publishing
A Michael Anderle Production

LMBPN Publishing
PMB 196, 2540 South Maryland Pkwy
Las Vegas, NV 89109

First US edition, July 2020
Version 1.01, July 2020
ebook ISBN: 978-1-64971-061-1
Print ISBN: 978-1-64971-062-8

THE RESISTANCE TO MAGIC TEAM

Thanks to our Beta Readers

Larry Omans, Mary Morris, Kelly O'Donnell, Nicole
Emens, Robert Brooks, Crystal Wren

Thanks to our JIT Readers

Veronica Stephan-Miller
Dorothy Lloyd
Dave Hicks
Diane L. Smith
Angel LaVey

Editor

SkyHunter Editing Team

CHAPTER ONE

Sariah inched her way through the chasm, sliding her body toward her goal. She screamed as a sharp piece of rock bit into her chest.

"*Damn* that hurts!"

She looked down. There was no blood and her shirt was intact, a good sign. She tried to angle her body to keep from impacting the rock further, but she was stuck. She'd either have to keep going and deal with the pain or make her way back.

Sariah sighed. She could call to the boys in the cavern behind her for help, but then she'd have to share whatever prize awaited her up ahead.

Her belly growled, reminding her she hadn't had a good meal in at least a day. Life was hard down in the mines, but it was better than dying in the streets or selling yourself in the sheets, so she made do.

Most of the kids in the town of Chatwick were miners, the only source of money in this godforsaken place. Some kids started as young as ten, going into the mine each day and foraging for their living.

Sariah had been lucky. Growing up with two living, working parents, she had been spared the grueling conditions of mine work.

As she neared adulthood and after her dad got injured, money grew scarce. So, here she was at sixteen, grinding out her days looking for veins of precious metals.

It wasn't all bad. When she found a good source, she was richly rewarded, and her tiny frame allowed her to reach spots others couldn't. She was quite good at it, too. Not that any of it would matter if she died stuck in this small crevasse.

Sariah laughed at herself, then stopped as the motion made the sharp piece of rock against her chest dig itself in further. She shook her head.

"Well, let's at least see if all this is gonna be worth it."

She wriggled her body around to free her hands, then carefully brought one hand down to her belt and unfastened her magitech lamp, and brought it forward to illuminate the path.

She squinted in the light as she tried to make out what lay ahead. The dim light glinted off the stone walls for a few more feet, then the walls gave way to a chamber. She couldn't make out any more, but if there was a chamber all the way down here, she knew something good would have to be in it.

With a stern expression, she gritted her teeth and pressed on and pushed forward as quickly as she could. The greedy bit of stone bit into her chest again as she moved, drawing precious drops of blood.

"Scheisse!" she yelped, but it was done. She was past the narrow spot.

Inwardly, she was glad her parents weren't there. They wouldn't approve of the swearing habit she'd picked up. The rearick were a rowdy bunch, and she enjoyed their company, but her parents thought they were a bad influence on her. They were probably right, but she didn't care.

She banished the thought and kept moving. The path grew wider as she went, and the stone started to get smoother, almost as if someone had already been through and leveled out the walls on purpose.

It didn't make any sense. Who would go through the hassle of digging out a chamber way down here, thousands of feet below the surface?

Her eyes took on the greedy look they got whenever she struck it big. Whoever it had been, they must have hidden something, and it was all hers now.

Walking got easier, and she thrust forward with bigger strides, waving her lamp before her in a wide arc to illuminate the walls.

In the distance, she caught a glimpse of something shiny in the wall. Throwing caution to the wind, she bounded the next few steps to close on the object.

She reached the end of the open chamber and stared at...nothing. The glint had been nothing more than the light reflecting off intricately carved lines on the wall. There was no ore to be found.

Sariah took one last furtive look at the bizarre pattern of lines scaling the walls. It had an unnatural look to it and almost looked like an animal.

Someone had carved the pattern intentionally, but she

couldn't very well move it out of the cavern, so it wouldn't pay the bills.

She started walking back toward the entrance and had only gone a few steps when she heard the crunch of boot on metal. She stopped and picked up the small object she had stepped on.

It was a pendant, and unlike anything she'd ever seen before. An ornate pattern of gold filigree curved around several decently sized gemstones of different varieties. The pattern made the shape of a small bird, perhaps a raven. It was hard to tell exactly. Two sapphires were in the place of its eyes, a diamond took over most of the body, and small garnets accented the points of the wings.

The pendant was breathtaking. Whoever had crafted it must have been a master.

Sariah wondered what the design meant and who would have left it there. In the end, it didn't matter, only how much it would sell for. The gemstones would fetch a good price once she dismantled the thing.

Hastily, she stuffed the pendant into her pack. It stuck out a little bit since her pack was already quite full. She hoped no one would notice because she didn't want to share her prize. No, she intended to claim this beauty all for herself.

Then she groaned as she remembered she'd have to get back through the narrow tunnel. She shrugged and decided to call upon the boys to help dig her out. They were always eager to help.

"Harvey! Padron!" She waited for a moment, but there was no answer. She walked back through the cavern until she was almost at the tight spot where she'd gotten stuck. "Harvey! Padron! I need help!" Still nothing.

Sariah had hoped the pleading tone in her voice would get them to come. Instead, she was staring at another empty chamber. She wondered if something was wrong. It wasn't like them to be completely quiet.

She called again another time or two with increasing volume, but it was useless. Gritting her teeth, she started working her way back through the crevasse. The tiny unforgiving piece of rock cut into her again, even harder this time.

"By the Matriarch!" she cried out as the stone cut into her breast anew. Then she was free. She looked down at the tears in her shirt and swore. She'd be forced to buy a new one, and shirts were expensive. Sariah hated spending money on such frivolities.

Back in the main corridor, she looked around for her friends, but they were nowhere to be found. In a state of almost panic, she spent several minutes looking for them before she realized how late it was, and they'd probably gone back home for dinner.

Her own belly growled at her again at the thought of food. "We'll eat soon," she told it. "I promise."

A small movement off to her left caught her eye. She looked over and focused harder, but just as quickly it was gone. The hairs on the back of her neck stood on end, and she readied for a confrontation.

"Boo!" a voice called out from behind her.

Sariah practically jumped out of her skin. She audibly yelped and spun around to face her new opponent, only to find Harvey playing a prank on her.

Harvey broke out into a boisterous laugh. "Got you!"

Sariah frowned and punched him in the arm. "Not funny. Quit sneaking up on me!"

His lips curled into a wide, toothy grin. "But you should have seen your face! That look was priceless."

Sariah glared at him. "Yeah, yeah. Is Padron hiding out there, too? Come out Padron, so I can deck you!"

"Nah, he headed back earlier." He pointed at her pack. "So, what's the haul? Find anything good back there?"

Her hand absentmindedly went to the bulge in her pack. Had he noticed? She hoped not. Her cheeks burned red, but in the dim light she figured he wouldn't notice.

Slowly, Sariah shook her head. "Nope, nothing. It was a dead end."

"Aww, man. Another night going hungry, I guess."

She felt bad for lying to him, but he'd get his own score soon enough. Besides, if the pendant was worth half what she thought it was, there'd be enough to share after she sold it.

The two made their way back to the elevator shaft in silence. When they reached the shaft, they found the platform had already been lowered, so they rode it up and out of the mine without incident.

The last few rays of sunshine greeted Harvey and Sariah as they made their way outside, weary and ready for food and sleep.

Sariah looked around for the foreman. He inspected everyone leaving the mines to make sure he got his due, but he was nowhere to be found. She shrugged. He must have gone home already, or more likely, to the bed of one of his mistresses.

She shivered in revulsion at the thought of what those women endured. As unforgiving as her mining career could be, it was a much better way to earn her pay.

Halfway to her house, she parted ways with Harvey. She waved to him and kept walking through the mostly empty streets.

After she was positive he was out of sight, she pulled the pendant out of her pack and stared at it. It was every bit as beautiful as before. She fingered the jewels, then put it back. It wouldn't do to walk around with something so valuable in full sight.

Sariah turned and headed toward the market square. She hoped she could find an appraiser tonight. She had precious few coins for food.

She wandered through several stalls but couldn't find what she was looking for. It was getting awfully dark, so this wasn't too shocking.

"Oh well," she muttered. "It can wait for tomorrow morning."

On her way back to her house, she stopped by a small fruit stand selling questionable, overripe options. She bought a few apples that had definitely seen better days with the last of her coins. She munched on one right away and saved the others for her parents. At least they wouldn't go completely hungry tonight.

As she trudged forward, a dark man watched her from the shadows of a nearby building. He had been following her unnoticed for some time.

His eyes darted to the bulge in the bag at her waist, then back to her. That was his quarry, all right.

He let her get more distance, then followed and took

great pains to ensure he wasn't seen by anyone. As he walked, his lips curled into a sinister smile.

Sariah woke with a start sometime after midnight. The air was cool and there was a breeze above her, which was odd because she usually kept her window closed. In the distance, she heard the howl of a lycanthrope on the prowl outside town.

At first, she thought maybe her growling tummy had woken her. One apple was hardly a sufficient meal.

Something about her room seemed…not quite right. She had the impression someone was in her room with her.

She cracked open her eyes and caught the pale glint of a knife hovering above her, poised to strike. With a yelp, she rolled out of the way as the knife descended, missing her head.

She quickly got to her feet and turned to face the threat. Her eyes widened in disbelief. The dagger appeared to hang in the air, moving as if on its own.

The knife came at her again. She lifted her blanket to use as a shield to block and slow its descent.

Sariah heard a muffled groan as the blade retracted. Her sleepy brain lit up with this new information. Maybe there was someone there after all, and not just an other-worldly knife moving on its own.

She lowered the blanket and leaped from her spot, shoulder lowered and out front. Her goal was to hit the midsection of where an attacker would be. Her shoulder connected with something hard, and both she and her assailant tumbled to the ground. As they fell, she heard the blade clatter as it fell.

Her attacker groaned again as he shoved Sariah's body off and scrambled away. Sariah tried to grab hold of something, but she still couldn't see him and was unable to find a purchase. Instead, she clambered up to her feet and got into a battle stance.

She glanced around the small room to determine what the would-be assassin would do next. The window behind her was open, but her door was not. It was unlikely her opponent would have made it past her, so he was most likely still in the room.

As if on cue, she heard more than saw the soft sound of metal clanking. Turning again, she saw the dagger lift in the air once more, pointed menacingly in her direction.

She cursed herself for forgetting the knife and rolled to dodge the incoming swipe.

This time she wasn't quite so lucky, and the blade sliced into her shoulder, making a sickening noise as it did so. She felt hot blood pour down her arm and instinctively shielded the wound with her other hand.

Sariah tried to think of her next move, but she was out of ideas. She had some experience fighting. The rearick in town were great fighters. They were all too eager to instruct others in the art, and she had been a willing student.

But it was very hard to hit someone you couldn't see. Escape was her best option.

She crept slowly around the room, keeping her eyes on the blade hanging in the air before her promising doom, until she found what she was looking for, the doorknob. She wrapped the hand on her injured arm around it and waited for the assassin to make his next move.

It didn't take long. A second later, her assailant lunged forward, aiming for her heart. She quickly turned the knob and practically fell out of the room, dodging the blade just in time.

Her attacker fell for the ruse and tumbled forward onto the ground again, though he managed to hold onto the blade this time.

Thinking fast, she kicked forward with all her might, aiming her feet for the blade's hilt. She heard the satisfying crunch of what sounded like bones as she made impact. The blade fell from her attacker's hands and she heard him swear loudly.

She lurched forward, managing to reach out with her good hand, hoping to connect with her attacker before he could regroup. This time, her hand felt something soft like linen. She grabbed onto it and pulled it toward her. As she did so, she could hear her assailant gasp in surprise.

She aimed for where she assumed the attacker's head would be and brought her own forehead to bear, trying to headbutt the man into submission. She ended up missing the head, but the full force of her skull impacted with something equally hard. The sound of wind rushed out of her attacker's lungs, and the man fell backward with enough force to tear the cloth in her hands.

Sariah got up to her feet and scrambled over to the dagger. She reached it and held it in front of her, hoping to ward off a further assault.

She glanced over at the fireplace. It had all but died out earlier on, but somehow now it was a raging inferno.

She could smell smoke from the fireplace fill her nostrils as the flames threatened to burn down the room. She raced back into her room to grab her blanket in an attempt to snuff out the flames, the attack all but forgotten amidst the new danger.

When she got back into the room, she saw the outline of a human in her doorway standing against the night. His eyes glowed bright white. She could make out some of the features of the attacker's face, but the fire in the room against the dark backdrop of night obscured most of her view.

The attacker seemed to salute her, then ducked out the doorway and into the street.

A moment later, the fire in the room died down. The scent of smoke disappeared entirely, and it was as if the fire had never happened.

Sariah cocked her head to the side and tried to make sense of what had just happened. She moved over to the fireplace and felt the stones. They were cool to the touch, and there were no burn marks anywhere, either.

"That's strange," she said to herself. She scratched her chin and pondered the bizarre turn of events. "Could it have been magic?"

She practically spat the last word, recalling the day her father had been hurt. Magic had been responsible then, and ever since she'd grown a serious distaste for the stuff.

Still, it would make sense. She'd heard tales of magicians who could make things appear out of thin air, or make people believe things that weren't true.

Most of those people were harmless, like the mystic who lived out in the forest a few days' walk from her town. Her father used to frequent the mystic before he became bedridden for various things.

If one of them were to use their powers for evil, anything was possible.

Sariah shook her head and walked back to her bedroom. She cradled the wound in her arm as she went. It was still oozing, and she was starting to feel dizzy from the blood loss.

Knowing she'd have to do something about it before too long, first she had to check on something. If an assassin had come for her in the night, he must have been after something of value.

Something like the pendant she'd retrieved from the mine today. Based on the timing, it was the only conclusion that made sense.

With her good hand, she reached under her bed and pulled out her work sack and rummaged through the contents. Her heart sank. The pendant was no longer there.

"Damn it!"

She wasn't sure how to track an invisible man, but now she had to go after him. The gems were her family's meal ticket for the next week at least, and as the grumble in her tummy reminded her, she hadn't eaten much in a while. Besides, he couldn't keep up his spell forever, and with the wounds she'd dealt him, he probably couldn't have gotten far.

She needed to do something about her wounded shoulder. She'd be of no use to anyone if she bled out on the way.

She stumbled across the room and rummaged through her shelves until she found a needle and some thread, then she headed back into the main room. She held the needle above the last smoldering coals of the fire to sterilize it, then gritted her teeth and got to work. Stitching her own wounds was a skill she'd learned a few years ago.

It wasn't uncommon to get scrapes and bruises when you grew up with rough friends like Harvey and Padron, and she didn't always want to tell her mother about them for fear of what she'd do to her, or worse, to them. She moved the needle quickly, favoring speed over precision, then tied off the thread and looked at her handiwork. It wasn't great, but it'd have to do.

She bounded toward the door, intent on catching her quarry before he could get out of town. The village was surrounded by a massive wall save for one gate, so she knew exactly where to go and what shortcuts to use to catch up to him.

As she crossed the threshold to her house, a thought came to her, unbidden. She wondered why her parents hadn't woken up amidst all the commotion downstairs. It didn't make sense. She'd made enough noise to wake half the town fending off her attacker.

A sinking feeling filled her gut. The assailant could wait. She had to check on her parents.

She raced up the stairs as fast as she could to her parents' bedroom. It was completely dark inside, but the familiar stench of blood filled her nostrils the moment she threw open the door.

Sariah felt like she was going to throw up, but she

steeled her stomach and went inside. If there was any chance her parents were alive, it was worth it.

She made her way over to the bed in the darkness and reached out a hand to touch her father's arm. It was still warm, but only barely. Reaching up to his neck, she hoped to feel a pulse, but there was none.

Instead, she felt a dark, sticky substance rub off on her fingers. She lifted them and sniffed. It was blood.

Quickly and with all hope fading, she moved over to check on her mother. She could barely bring herself to feel around for her mother, but when she did, she found the same slit across her throat.

Tears welled up in her eyes. Her parents, her whole world, were dead. And the magic assassin was to blame.

Sariah couldn't hold it back any longer. Her stomach lurched and heaved its meager contents onto the ground. She felt the taste of acid in her mouth as she fell backward and collapsed against the wall.

The tears came in earnest, and she let out all her feelings and sobbed. The night's happenings were too much for her to handle.

As she laid there and cried, covered in her parents' blood, she thought about the assassin. She wasn't sure how, but she knew she'd have to find him.

And she would make him pay.

CHAPTER TWO

Harvey tugged on the corners of the sleeves of his best shirt. In Chatwick, people rarely put on their good clothes for fear of getting them dirty. They only wore them for special occasions and not a moment longer, so the shirt was stiff around the edges and about a size too small.

He wriggled his shoulders, trying to make the shirt fit better, but it made no difference. No matter, he would take it back off again soon enough.

Turning, Harvey saw his reflection in the mirror and took a long, hard look at his appearance. Strands of his thick, black hair were sticking out of the top of his head at an odd angle, and there was a small amount of fresh stubble on his chin. A small scar under his left eye from a mining accident a few weeks ago marred his otherwise clear, flawless skin.

He didn't have enough time to shave, but he wet down one hand with some saliva and used it to slick the hair back in place. He shrugged. He didn't consider himself much of a looker, and it would have to do for now.

He was just delaying the inevitable. Maybe if he never left the house, he wouldn't have to face the realities of today, and the awful event of three days ago had never really happened.

Who was he kidding? It had happened, and now he had to go and console his best friend on the worst day of her life.

As he walked out the door, the sun hit him right in the face. It was bright today, far brighter than it had been recently. He had to squint to block out the sun's rays well enough to see.

Was this some sort of cruel trick of the Matriarch and Patriarch, to have the weather be amazing on a day so terrible? he wondered. No, that was unfair. He was just sour.

A few minutes later, he found his friend Sariah. She was sitting on a stool next to the town priest and their other friend, Padron. The migrant rearick was trying to tell an off-color joke to lighten the mood, but he didn't catch the words.

"Hey," Harvey called out.

Sariah lifted her face to meet his. Her eyes were puffy and swollen with dark circles underneath. It looked like she hadn't slept in days. Not that he could blame her. He'd reacted in a similar manner when his mom had passed.

She'd died of the wasting sickness. There was nothing anyone could have done. Harvey had been near-inconsolable then, and Sariah had been his rock during that hard time. She'd comforted him and helped him come to terms with his new reality. Harvey could only hope he would be just as good a friend to her now as she had been to him then.

"Hey," Sariah replied at last. "Glad you could finally make it."

He knew her words held no malice to them, but they still made him wince. She was right, he should have been there sooner.

Sariah noticed his reaction and her face softened. "I didn't mean it like-"

"I know," Harvey cut her off. "It's okay. Today is going to be hard for you. I'm the one who should apologize for being late."

"No, it's okay. You're fine. I'm just glad you're here to support me." She stood up and placed a hand on his shoulder.

Harvey made a broad sweeping motion to encompass the crowd. "And miss all this? Wouldn't dream of it." He gave her a wink.

Sariah snickered and her lips turned upward into a smile. "With moves like that, you must be a hit with all the girls."

Harvey winced. He supposed he'd deserved that. He was about to make a witty reply but was interrupted by the town priest, Jackson, who got up and offered him his seat. Harvey was quick to oblige.

Jackson walked forward to the two fresh holes in the ground before them. Each one held a small urn containing the remains of Sariah's mother and father.

Cremation was standard practice in this part of the world. It took far fewer resources and a lot less space to burn the bodies than it did to bury them whole in caskets.

Only the richest of the rich could afford such luxury, and no one in Chatwick had that kind of money, not even the foreman.

Harvey felt like his friends' parents deserved better, not that he could do anything about it now.

He looked at Sariah and gave her a brief smile. She looked back at him with a sad expression on her face and held out a hand. He took it and squeezed, then focused on the priest's speech. He wondered what the man would say this time.

The priest called for everyone to be silent so he could start the ceremony, then began talking about the cycle of life and how everyone was important, but Sariah wasn't really listening.

She was in her own head, battling her own internal demons. She had been fortunate to grow up with both her parents in a loving household. It was a comfort not many knew, and she should feel fortunate.

Even after the accident, when her father got injured, he had been around for her, there to talk to about her hopes and fears, or whatever new thing happened in the mines that was interesting. Few days passed without something of note to share.

Tears started to fall from her cheeks, tracing small lines down her face as they fell to the ground. For a moment, Sariah felt like she was one of those tears, hurtling along a set path toward a lackluster and meaningless end.

She looked over at Padron. He was giving her one of his

big, goofy grins. She smiled back at him weakly. He was trying to cheer her up the only way he knew how.

That was the way with the group of rearick in town. They'd migrated here from a place called The Heights several years ago. They said it was a very happy place, and never dwelled on bad times for too long. Whenever something bad happened, they'd say their peace and then tell jokes to lighten the mood. Normally, she found their gallows humor hilarious, but today it fell on deaf ears.

Guess it's true, she thought. Things really are different when you're the one affected.

She looked back at Jackson. He was still in the middle of his spiel, spouting off something about how the Matriarch and Patriarch had a plan for everyone and how even seemingly terrible things fit into their plan.

Sariah snorted in disgust. She had tried to keep it quiet but failed miserably. Everyone stared at her. Even Jackson stopped speaking to see if she was all right. She waved everyone off with a hand and a barely audible "Sorry."

The priest nodded once and went back to his speech.

She blushed. She hated making a scene or being the center of attention, and here she was, doing both. Today royally sucked on multiple counts.

Jackson reached the end of his sermon. "Would anyone like to say a few words?" he asked the assembly.

Would I ever. I'd love to say a few things about how unfair all of this is and how your stupid sermon doesn't help anyone, she thought. That's what she wanted to shout until her lungs were raw and her face turned blue.

She stayed quiet. What good would an emotional outburst do for anyone? It wouldn't bring her parents back, and all it would do is upset the guests. No, she had to keep it together. She always kept it together.

The town priest looked expectantly out at those gathered. He started to shuffle his feet. It was just a little motion, barely perceptible, but it was there. If Sariah hadn't been busy trying to pay attention to anything but what was actually going on, she probably would have missed it.

Finally, someone stood up. It was Molly. She had been a friend of Sariah's mother for several years. Molly told stories of their shared history, about swapping recipes and child-rearing advice, playdates, things of that nature. It was sweet. Too sweet, but nice all the same.

Another person, someone Sariah didn't recognize, got up to give a speech. Like the priest, their words were about finding purpose and meaning in dark times like this one.

Sariah bowed her head so no one could see her face and sneered. What does he know, anyway?

If there was anything she'd taken away from the attack on her house and parents, it was the pointlessness of existence. She kept going over the night in her head, but the whole thing made no sense.

Why had the assassin killed her parents? She couldn't come up with a good answer.

She could understand why he stole the pendant, it had value. Maybe it had even been originally his. That part made sense.

She could even understand his desire to kill her, no witnesses and all that, and no one left to lay a claim to the goods. But why had he gone after her parents? They were innocent. She hadn't even told them about her find yet. It was a senseless act of violence.

Tears came anew then, and she was glad her face wasn't visible. She didn't want more pity from these people. What she wanted was revenge and some semblance of justice for her parents' deaths.

Her resolve had not weakened. Sariah wasn't quite sure where to start, but she was determined not to let the fiend get away with it. She would track him to the ends of Irth if need be.

As thoughts of revenge replaced ones of sadness, her face darkened and she clenched her fists so hard she drew blood. The feel of wet blood on her hands brought her attention back to reality.

Slowly, she relaxed her hands. They were shaky at first and it took a moment for them to stop. She wiped the droplets of blood off on her black dress.

At least no one will see the stains, she thought wryly. She laughed a little in spite of herself and spared a look at Padron. Maybe his brand of humor had worn off on her more than she thought.

***

The funeral ended a short while later, and Sariah's parents were buried under fresh mounds of dirt, where the last of their mortal remains would stay until the end of days.

Everyone had said their condolences to Sariah and left. Everyone but Harvey and Padron. They sat next to their grieving friend, unsure of what to say or do.

The sky was starting to get dark. Harvey needed to get

back to his house soon or his father would be worried about him. Then he felt guilty because Sariah no longer had parents to worry about her.

"It's, umm, going to be okay, you know. Eventually," Harvey muttered after what felt like an hour's silence.

Sariah scowled, making him instantly regret the words. He cursed himself for his poor timing. He was always saying the wrong thing at the wrong time.

"I'm sorry," she blurted out. "I shouldn't have scowled at you."

Harvey let out a nervous laugh. "No, it's my fault. I had my foot in my mouth." He made some hand motions like he was trying to stuff his foot into his mouth and gag on it.

Sariah giggled at the sight. Harvey could be bull-headed, but he knew how to cheer her up when it mattered. "It's okay. I know you were only trying to help."

"Is there anything we can do fer ya tonight, lass?" Padron asked. There was an uncharacteristically worried look on his brow as he spoke.

Sariah shook her head. "No, it's okay. I still have some cleanup to do at home."

Padron shot up. "Ye should let us do that fer ya. Don't ya lift a finger tonight, and I'll bring meself over first thing in the morning to take care of it all for ya."

Sariah made a dismissive gesture with her hands. "That's really sweet of you to offer, but really, I don't need any help."

Padron frowned and practically glared at her. "I won't hear it. We'll help ya out, with whatever ya need. Promise. It's the least we can do."

Sariah smiled up at him. "Okay, if you insist."

Harvey looked at her. Something was wrong, though he couldn't put his finger on it. She had agreed to Padron's help way too easily.

Sariah had always been a do-it-yourself type of girl, believing you should make your own way in life. That's why she'd headed to the mines willingly when her father had been injured a while back.

He let it slide. Today had been very emotional for all of them. Maybe she was just tired from the strain. Yes, he decided, that must be it.

Sariah stood. "I should really get going. I don't want to keep you two longer than necessary."

Harvey stood as well and moved to block her path. "At least let me walk you home or something," he insisted. Sariah started to argue, but he silenced it with a motion of his hand. "Please. Plus, now I'm really curious about how big of a mess we're going to have to clean up tomorrow," he added with a dopey grin.

She looked him in the eyes for a few seconds, then nodded slowly. "How can a girl turn down a tempting offer like that?"

He smiled even broader. "That's what I was hoping you'd say."

Sariah gave him an odd look like he was messing up some hidden plan of hers, but he dismissed it. The day had worn on both of them. Instead, he extended an arm, which she readily accepted. Then the two said their goodbyes to Padron and went about their way.

As they walked, Harvey looked up at the sky. The stars were starting to come out and the moon was about half-full, providing a decent amount of light. During any other circumstance, it would have been like something out of a picture, but tonight it didn't feel right.

He looked at Sariah. The moon was reflected in her dark green eyes, making them look surreal. He cleared his throat, then blushed and turned away.

What do you say to a friend who had lost her parents? he wondered. He tried to think of what she'd told him years ago, but nothing came to mind.

No matter what he thought of saying, none of it seemed adequate. He chided himself again for acting like a fool. What was he doing with her now, anyway? Why'd he offer to walk her home if he was only going to shut down? He was a moron.

Finally, Sariah broke the awkward silence. "I'm not sure what I'm going to do," she admitted.

"Er, about what?"

"About everything. I don't know how I can even keep the house after this, let alone eat. What am I going to do without my family?" Another tear was streaking down her soft cheek.

Harvey felt even more the fool. Here he was, worrying about his own stupid thoughts when the weight of the world was crushing his friend's shoulders.

"I hadn't really thought about that."

Sariah blushed and turned away from him. "I'm sorry, I shouldn't be bugging you about this."

"No, it's okay. Promise."

Sariah started walking again, but Harvey grabbed her arm to stop her. He turned her around until she was looking at him. "Hey. Listen to me. You don't need to apologize for anything, you understand?" His tone was serious, which was unusual for him.

She stared into his brown eyes. "I understand. It's just, what if this is a sign? Maybe I'm not supposed to stay here."

A look of concern crossed Harvey's face. "You're not honestly thinking of going after the assassin, are you?"

Sariah rolled her eyes. They'd had this argument before, the day after the attack. "Maybe. I mean, what's left for me here now, anyway?"

Harvey scoffed. "You can't honestly be asking that question, can you? You still have friends here, like Padron and me. We'll take care of you."

"I don't want to be a burden on either of you." She looked away.

Harvey shook his head. "You wouldn't be. We can figure it out. Please, tell me you'll think about it, okay? It's a dangerous world out there and you've never even been outside the walls of town once."

She didn't want to admit it, but he had a point. She had no idea where to go or what to do outside of the relative comfort of the town. It was likely a suicide mission to go out there, but that didn't dampen her resolve one bit.

"I'll think about it," she conceded.

A big smile crossed Harvey's lips. "Good. Now let's get you home."

The two resumed walking and made it the rest of the way in silence. When they reached the house, Harvey insisted he sleep in the main room of her house for her protection. It was really to keep her from doing something rash or stupid.

Sariah put up quite a fight but eventually relented.

Harvey could be quite stubborn when he made up his mind about something.

She made up a bed for him on the couch with a couple spare blankets and went off to her room to sleep. Harvey stayed up until he was sure she got to sleep, then exhaustion claimed him as well.

Early the next morning, Sariah made up her mind. She would leave today. She couldn't bear to be a burden on her friends any more than she already had been, and thoughts of revenge burned bright in her heart.

She crept around her room and packed travel supplies into her bag as quietly as she could. Harvey was a light sleeper, and if he woke up he'd do something stupid like insist on going with her.

That was the last thing she wanted. There was no need to involve someone else in her quest. No one else had been attacked and had their future robbed. Just her. She would make the trip on her own. It was better that way.

Fortunately, she didn't have to do much to prepare. She'd spent a good portion of the last few days going through her parents' things scrounging for needed supplies.

Sariah looked at the meager contents of her pack. She had a sleeping roll and blanket, a canteen, changes of clothes, some rope, a hammer, the knife the assassin had used, and a few pieces of her mother's jewelry she hoped she could barter for supplies.

She looked at the knife. Its handle was ornate with an

odd design on it, but aside from flecks of blood still clinging to the blade like a monument to her parents' deaths, it could have passed for an ordinary knife. She cursed the assassin in her head. Perhaps one day soon, she'd get to use it on him to end his life in a similar manner. The thought gave her a glimmer of hope.

She pushed the blade deep into the pack so she didn't have to look at it. She'd need it eventually, but for now it was better if it stayed out of sight.

There was one notable thing missing from her pack. She had no food, something she was just going to have to figure out along the way. If she'd asked any of her friends for several days of food, it would have looked suspicious.

She was fairly confident in her ability to scrounge for vittles once she got out in the wild. Like any self-respecting denizen of Chatwick, Sariah had seen plenty of lean days where food from the forests around the village was all that was available. She could identify edible plants easily enough.

That left only one item left to pack, an old map of the area. Her father had kept it hanging on one of his walls, at least since she was born. She had no way of knowing how current it was, but the landscape couldn't have changed much.

In her younger days, she'd always thought the map was a waste of good paper. After all, they never went anywhere, but now, it could end up being the single most important thing she packed.

She hefted the bag and secured it to her shoulders. It was heavy but manageable. She probably wouldn't be able to make very good time with it, but her next destination was only about two days' march away.

Slowly, Sariah opened the door and took a furtive glance at her living room. She couldn't see Harvey directly from this angle, but the blankets she'd laid out for him were still strewn about the couch.

She opened the door the rest of the way. It made a slight creaking noise, and she cringed, but no movement came from the room in front of her.

Creeping as softly as she could, she inched forward and crossed the living room as quickly as she could, not even daring to glance in Harvey's direction on the off chance doing so would somehow wake him.

A few more strides and she made it to the front door. She allowed herself to breathe a small sigh of relief before she opened it only to find a tall figure blocking her way.

"Thought you'd sneak off without me?" Harvey's voice boomed. He had a giant, dopey grin on his face. He was obviously quite pleased with himself for figuring out her plan.

"You big oaf! You're not going to dissuade me!" She punched him on the shoulder.

Harvey rubbed the point of impact. "Of course not. That's why I decided to go with you."

She caught sight of the pack he had tied to his own back. It looked pretty similar to hers. Apparently, he'd been busy, too.

Sariah sighed. It was the last thing she wanted, but she knew there was little point in arguing with him. Harvey was every bit as pig-headed and stubborn as she was.

She'd have to try and lose him somewhere on the path

while they were still close enough to the village for him to turn back. She groaned. That wasn't a very nice fate for her friend. Maybe she could ditch him somewhere safer.

At last, she relented. "Fine. You can come. But only so far as our first stop. And if you slow me down in any way, I won't hesitate to leave you behind. Got it?"

Harvey gulped down a lump in his throat. "You got it, boss." He grinned at her again. "Shall we?"

Sariah rolled her eyes. Somewhere deep inside, she was glad for the company, though she wouldn't admit it to Harvey. He'd never let her live it down if she did.

"Let's get moving before the rest of the town hears your booming voice and wakes up," she replied. She stormed past him and started for the town gate, not bothering to look to see if he was following.

Harvey ran to catch up. "Wait!" he cried. "Where are we even going?"

Sariah turned on her heels. She looked up into his eyes and gave him a wry smile of her own. "Maybe you should have thought of that before you signed on to this trip."

Harvey whined. He had walked right into that one. He motioned for her to keep going with one of his hands. "Lead the way, my lady."

Her eyes practically beamed at him. She liked the feeling of knowing something he didn't. "Oh, I will."

CHAPTER THREE

Lucien's eyes darted around cautiously. He was extra careful to make sure no one followed him. Not that anyone ever did.

He excelled at hiding, even employing magic to aid on occasion, but today he wasn't using such tricks. He'd need all the mental fortitude he could muster for the confrontation to come.

Taking another look behind himself to triple-check he was alone, he breathed a sigh of relief and let himself rest for a moment against the side of a nearby building.

He inhaled deeply, and his ribs stung where that bitch of a girl had kicked him a few days prior. He reached out with his bandaged hand, another of the bitch's gifts, and rubbed the sore spot. He replayed the incident in his mind.

It had been a simple job, or at least, it was supposed to be simple. But the snatch and grabs, somehow they were never as easy as they looked.

Lucien should have known something was up when his master sent him to the backwater town of Chatwick. Why anyone would want to go to that blasted place on purpose, he would never know.

The mission had been straightforward enough. Retrieve a small artifact left there by accident and bring it back, no questions asked, and kill anyone who found out about it, of course. No witnesses. One can never have witnesses in his line of work.

It had gone nice and smoothly for the most part, too. Until that little slip of a girl woke up and somehow managed to get the drop on him.

He only had himself to blame. He never should have left the knife visible, but he enjoyed toying with his victims. With his mental magic, he could have hidden everything, including the blade, but he liked to leave some part of himself visible to his victims. It was his trademark move to let them see just a hint, a sliver of their impending doom. He got off on the thrill of seeing their fear-filled expressions.

If he'd been more cautious and hidden everything, that little bitch never would have stood a chance.

There was no point in worrying about it all now. He had the item he'd been asked to find, and there was no chance a hick girl from backwaterville was going to do anything about it anyway.

All that was left was informing the Master about the job and returning the goods. Which was why he was here, on the outskirts of the complex.

He rubbed the sore spot on his chest again. If he didn't know better, he'd swear one of his ribs was cracked. For a moment, he wished he could heal the wound so he'd be in top shape for the upcoming meeting. Alas, such magical power eluded him.

There were a few people, like the Master, who could perform those feats, but to ask for help, he'd have to admit his partial failure, and that wasn't going to happen if he could avoid it.

Lucien spat on the ground in disgust and got moving. There was no point in delaying the inevitable any further. It wouldn't change the outcome.

He took a couple more glances around to make sure no one else was in the vicinity. Satisfied he was well and truly alone, he approached a run-down looking building in front of him.

The building was unassuming, save for a raven symbol etched into the otherwise normal door. Even the raven itself had been designed in such a way as to make it not stand out. Passersby would never notice it unless they knew what to look for, which was a good thing for all involved.

He ungloved his right hand and tapped on the door a half dozen times in quick succession. The taps formed a unique pattern, like notes in a song.

For a moment, nothing happened, then a tiny opening formed in the doorway. No eyes greeted him, nor was there any indication someone was on the other side, but Lucien knew better.

He placed his hand over the opening, palm forward so the onlooker could inspect it. On his palm was a tiny tattoo, practically hidden among the other creases and lines, of a raven expanding its wings. It was the only outward sign he was a member of the order, and the only marking they all shared.

Nothing happened for a solid minute while he held his open palm up against the door. This was part of the challenge, too. Not only did a member need to have the right marking on their hand, but the gatekeepers needed to verify the person at the door was an active member. Otherwise, the punishment would be swift and sure.

He'd never heard of anyone leaving the organization through any means but death, so he wasn't really sure why it was necessary, but he obeyed the rules, in no hurry to make his own exit from this world.

After a few moments, he heard a shuffling noise on the other side of the door, and the tiny opening closed, then creaked and groaned as it was pulled open, allowing him to enter.

"Nice to see you again, Master Lucien," the gate guard, Daniel, said to him.

Lucien scoffed. "Yeah, nice to see you too."

"The Master has been expecting you. I trust you have good news to share?"

It wasn't so much a question as a statement. One didn't bother returning from their missions unless they were successful. The Master didn't tolerate failure at any level.

"Of course, Daniel. Can we drop the charade already? I'd like to get back out there as soon as possible."

An eerie light glinted in Daniel's eyes. "Yes sir, Master Lucien. Right this way."

Daniel pointed down the hallway and started walking. Lucien followed, making sure to stay close for fear of getting lost.

Lucien had been to see the Master once before, but that didn't mean he knew where he was going. The complex was a veritable rat's nest of rooms and passageways flung together in random, maddening patterns that took them deep underground. He was pretty sure it had been built in such a way on purpose to foil would-be invaders.

The Master also never held court in the same room twice. Only a select few, like Daniel, knew where he was going to be on a given day. Going to the same location he'd been to the last time, even if he felt confident he could find it, would be futile.

After several minutes of navigating the tunnels, some of which Lucien was sure went in circles, they arrived at a wooden door.

Daniel scraped and bowed, then turned and walked away, leaving Lucien on his own.

Lucien let out a dry laugh. He wondered for a moment how he'd get back to the entrance but pushed the thought far from his mind. It wouldn't do to be thinking such things in front of the Master. One could show no weaknesses of any kind.

Tentatively, he pushed open the door. The room beyond was dimly lit by a single torch on the far wall. The light barely illuminated the single, robed figure.

The figure beckoned him to move forward into the light. Lucien obliged.

He knelt on the ground. "Master, I have completed the task you laid out for me and have come bearing the pendant."

The robed figure pushed his hood back, revealing his face.

Lucien gasped. The man standing before him was undoubtedly the Master, but he looked nothing like he had the last time. He'd spoken to a younger man with a shock of blonde hair and clear, tanned skin. The man now had black hair graying at the edges, dark blue eyes, and a massive scar running down the left side of his face into the corner of his mouth. It was a frightening sight.

He'd heard rumors the Master was a changeling, someone who could take on another's appearance at will. More likely, he was using mental magic. Mental magic could do many wondrous things, including reading another's thoughts and making someone think you were someone else.

It was a clever plan. Since no one knew the Master's true name or appearance, he could never be brought to justice on the off chance someone caught him. In fact, there was no way to know it was even really a "him."

The Master smiled down at Lucien, setting him at ease. "Thank you, my child," he answered. The Master reached out. "Please surrender the artifact."

Lucien nodded. "Of course, Master." He rummaged around in his pockets and produced the pendant. It was every bit as gorgeous as it had been when Sariah had found it in the mine.

Eagerly, the Master ripped the pendant out of Lucien's outstretched hand. He brought it up and inspected it with a critical eye.

"Did I ever tell you why this pendant is so important to me?" the Master asked him.

Lucien shook his head. "No, Master." Inwardly, he wondered why the Master was even asking him about it.

The man wasn't known for talking about anything but work with his underlings.

"It's a very old piece. From before the Age of Madness, even. It has been in my family for generations."

"That sounds very important, Master." Lucien was confused but went along.

The Master stared intently at the pendant for another few seconds, then turned his attention back to his servant. "Were there any complications on the mission?"

Lucien lowered his gaze. He started to reply, then felt a foreign presence at the edge of his mind. A mild pain came with it. He wanted to clutch the sides of his head to make it go away but remained stalwart.

It quickly became obvious to him the Master was burrowing into his brain. Lucien desperately tried to clear his mind and block out his thoughts. He must not let the Master find out the truth.

"N-n-no, Master," Lucien stammered. Sweat formed on his brow as he spoke the lie out loud.

The Master's smile turned downwards into a frown as the pressure on Lucien's head evaporated. "I see. Is that all there is to report?"

Lucien trembled in fear. He wasn't sure if it would be worse to admit partial failure or be caught in a lie. He chose the latter. "Yes, Master. The pendant has been returned in one piece, and the witnesses were dealt with swiftly and surely."

The Master's eyes narrowed and grew cold. "Now Lucien, you are not being completely honest with me, are you?"

Lucien swallowed hard. His whole body was sweating

now. He looked up into the Master's eyes. "Actually, sir, there was…this girl."

The Master held out his free hand and patted Lucien on the shoulder. "Yes, my child. I know. I have seen it all. She bested you in the middle of the night, injuring you and forcing a hasty retreat. Quite pathetic, really."

Lucien's eyes went wide. How could the Master have possibly known? Then it hit him. The Master must be reading his very thoughts.

He groaned and hung his head in shame and fear, which only worsened his mood.

The corners of the Master's lips expanded in a broad grin. The sound of his laughter filled the chamber. "Do not be afraid, child. I am not quite so cruel as the tales would have you believe."

Lucien looked back up at him. "Y-you're not?"

The Master placed his free hand under Lucien's chin and lifted his head up a little more, then squatted down until they were practically eye to eye. "No, child." There was a lightness, almost like a laugh, in his tone. "If I killed every servant who made the slightest error, I would have no more servants to rely on. That would be bad for business."

"Thank you!" Lucien breathed a massive sigh of relief.

"But." The Master's eyes narrowed once more, making a knot of fear form in Lucien's gut. "I still need results. Surely, you can understand that."

"You needn't worry about that little bitch of a girl, Master." Lucien worked to steady his voice as he spoke. "She's a nobody. There ain't a soul alive she could tell about us even if she wanted to."

The Master straightened. He rubbed his chin thoughtfully for a second. "Hmm. You may be right. But that is only one of your problems."

Lucien's terror grew. "One?" he said shakily.

The Master thrust the pendant forward until the medallion was practically up against Lucien's eyeballs. "Look here. The pendant is missing two of its gemstones. They must have fallen out in your little scuffle."

"Impossible!" Lucien couldn't be sure. Studying the object carefully, he could indeed see two indentations where sapphires should have been.

He bowed his head once more in shame. His failure had been more complete than even he knew. He wasn't sure what punishment would be in store for him, but he feared the worst.

"Forgive me, Master. I had no idea."

The Master grinned again, showing off his teeth. "Oh, I will do better than that child. I'm going to give you a chance to redeem yourself."

Lucien's fear started to dissipate, and he smiled in spite of himself. "Thank you, Master. You are too generous."

"You will return to Chatwick, to the little girl's house, and you will recover the missing gemstones."

Lucien nodded fervently.

"And you will silence the girl, along with anyone she may have come in contact with."

Lucien's jaw dropped. "But Master, who knows how many people in town she could have told about it by now?"

The Master was unfazed. "And? Silence the whole town if you need to. No one will notice. It's a tiny backwater place."

The casual tone with which the Master spoke chilled Lucien to the bone. Had he really ordered the extermination of a whole town over this slight? That was a bit much, even for Lucien. Just who was he working for?

He quickly distanced those thoughts from his head. They would not serve him well here, not when the Master could read them.

"Am I understood, child?" the Master asked. "Or do I need to find another use for you?"

Lucien shuddered. He was hesitant to agree to such a heinous task, but he eventually nodded. He would not fail twice. "Yes, Master. I promise I shall not fail you again."

The Master laughed at the small man kneeling before him. "Of course not, child. I am gracious with my second chances. But know this. There is no such thing as a third. Not in my house."

There was no mistaking the threat. Lucien would find a way to accomplish his task this time, or the Master would have him killed. Or worse, use him in one of his magical experiments.

Not much was known about the experiments the Master performed with his victims, only it was severely painful, and no one was ever the same afterward if they were unfortunate enough to survive at all. The fear of the unknown was enough to strengthen his resolve.

The Master made a dismissive gesture with his free hand. "Now leave. Daniel will see you out."

Lucien stood up, and left. As he walked out of the room and closed the door behind him, he began to instantly feel better. The fear left him, and he stopped sweating as his body cooled to a normal temperature.

He wondered if the Master intentionally made the rooms hotter than normal to put his guests off guard. It was a smart strategy if it were true, and one he could respect.

He looked around for the gatekeeper. He didn't have to wait long. Daniel came around the corner, almost as if he had been waiting there the whole time.

The two made their way out of the complex in silence. Lucien was lost in thought. He wasn't sure how a stupid girl had gotten the better of him the last time they met, but he damn sure wasn't going to let it happen again.

The man known only as the Master smiled as he watched his little assassin leave. He looked down at the small pendant in his hand and let out a slight laugh.

It had been his fault he'd left it down in the mine in the first place. He'd never imagined someone would stumble upon it before he could get a man in there to retrieve it. It was downright insane the way everything had played out, almost like the Bitch and Bastard were playing tricks on him.

No matter, he'd sent a very capable man to complete the job, and he was quite certain Lucien would get it right this time. He had lots of tricks up his sleeve, having been a fantastic student of his magical teachings, unlike so many others.

Speaking of others, it was time to go check on his little pet projects. He made his way out of the darkened room and started roaming the hallways. He was in no particular hurry. The people he was on his way to see weren't going anywhere.

After several minutes, he came to an iron door. It was the only reinforced door inside the complex. He brought forth a tiny key from one of his pockets and after unlocking it made his way inside.

The room was dark, but he clapped his hands and several magitech lights hummed as they came to life. Magitech was hard to come by in this part of Irth, and few had more than a couple pieces of it. He had several, of course, though he used them sparingly.

The people chained to the far wall groaned when the lights came on. They knew what it meant. The lights only came on when the Master was ready to play.

He walked up to the first chained man. The poor fellow's face was gaunt and stretched. His lips trembled and his body shook in fear.

"Hello Charles," the Master said through grinning teeth. "Are you ready for our little experiment?"

Charles tried to look away but couldn't. A second later, the screams started. It was a long time before they stopped.

CHAPTER FOUR

Sariah stared down at her map with a look of consternation. She and Harvey had been traveling for over a day, heading west in what she assumed was the right direction.

She couldn't really tell, though. Map reading wasn't a skill she'd ever picked up. Why bother, when you don't go anywhere in the first place? That's what she'd told herself growing up. Now she was wishing she'd spent more time listening to her father drone on about it.

The sun was high overhead in the sky. She had to squint against the glare to see the tiny cabin marked out on her map. It was the only structure not a town or a village, and it was their destination.

"Need help?" Harvey asked, looking over her shoulder.

Sariah jumped. His interruption had startled her. Hastily, she folded the map and turned and glared at him. "What business do you have startling me like that?"

Harvey shrugged. "Sorry. Can't help it, I guess."

"I don't need any help," Sariah insisted. "I know what I'm doing."

He eyed her suspiciously. "Is that so?"

"Yes, it is."

It was a bald-faced lie, of course, but she wasn't about to admit that to him. She was still mad at her friend for inserting himself into her trip to begin with. It was petty, she knew, but she wasn't above it.

Still, she thought, maybe it wouldn't be so bad to have him help out.

Sariah glanced at her friend. He was grinning like a madman and giving her an odd look. She quickly determined it wasn't worth the risk. If she let him help her now, she'd never hear the end of it.

Little Sariah, lost in the woods, not even two days' travel away from their village. She could almost hear the jeers Harvey and Padron would heap upon her when they got back. The thought was enough to make her shudder.

"I know exactly where we're going," she lied again. "All we need to do is keep heading west and we should reach our destination before nightfall."

Harvey still had a dopey grin on his face. "And just where is this destination of ours again, anyway?"

Sariah smirked at him. "You'll have to wait and see." She lightly patted his cheek with one of her hands like she was patronizing a child.

Nope, definitely not above being petty. Not with Harvey, at least

Harvey frowned at her. "Come on. Haven't I proven myself by now?"

"What do you mean?" She sighed. "I didn't even ask you to come to begin with!"

"Sure, but you're glad I did, right? I mean, you didn't

even have any food on you when you left. You would have gone hungry last night without me around, and it's safer to travel in numbers."

This time it was Sariah who frowned. He did have a point. Harvey had brought ample food supplies with him, enough for both of them for a week. She had no idea what he had to do to get his hands on so much, but it must have been hard.

In spite of her hopes, she hadn't been able to find much edible last night. Apparently, the further out you got into the woods, the harder it was to find things. His food stores had indeed come in handy.

At last, she relented. "All right, I suppose you've earned a tiny hint."

"That's more like it." There was that dopey grin again. "So? Where are we going?"

"We're going to a cabin in the woods." She smirked at him again. She knew the clue was deceptively vague.

"Oh, come on. Not even a proper hint?" Harvey shook his head. "What did I do to deserve this?"

"It's more like what didn't you do," she replied cryptically.

Harvey opened his mouth to say something but shut it just as quickly. The sound of a low howl a short distance away made them both stop in their tracks.

There was no telling what the sound might be coming from. It could be anything from a lone wolf to a lycanthrope out for blood. One thing was for sure, neither of them wanted to find out.

Sariah placed a finger on her lips, telling Harvey to be quiet. He nodded in agreement.

She crouched low to the ground and motioned for Harvey to do the same, then looked around their little clearing, eyes darting in every direction.

The two were completely still for a couple of moments, but nothing more happened. There were no further howls and no sense of anything moving in their general vicinity.

Sariah let out a deep sigh of relief. It seemed they would be safe enough for now. She dug through her pack and got out the knife, tucking it into her belt. She still hated looking at it, but she no longer wanted it to be out of reach, either.

If anything did attack them, she wanted to be prepared. Harvey followed her lead, securing two of his own knives in a similar fashion, one on each side of his body.

She looked at the two of them crouched there on the ground, afraid of a distant howl and armed with nothing but a couple of daggers. It was disheartening.

What are we even doing, she wondered. The two of them had never seen real combat. Only scuffles and rough-housing around the streets of the town. They'd both be worthless in a real fight.

Maybe she should head back now before she got too lost to find her way. No one would think any less of her, except for Harvey. He might, but she didn't really care about his opinion anyway.

Harvey stood and offered her a hand. She accepted and stood as well. Her eyes caught his, and she stared into them.

Harvey's eyes had a gentleness to them, but there was something else there, too. Loyalty, maybe, or something more akin to faith.

At that moment, she knew with certainty Harvey had no doubt she could complete her quest. His unshakable faith restored a bit of her own self-confidence, and she knew just how to repay it.

Sariah bent over and picked up her father's map, which she'd dropped earlier amid the fear and confusion. She dusted it off and opened it back up.

"Okay, you win," she told Harvey. She shoved the map in his direction. "I have no idea how to read one of these things. Please, help me out."

Harvey's lips curled upwards into a big, goofy grin. "I'd be only too happy to do so, milady," he said with a slight bow.

He tugged on the map. "Now, show me where our destination is."

Sariah pointed at a small house surrounded by trees with one grubby finger. "Here."

Harvey had to squint to see where she was pointing. "The mystic's hut?" he asked, confused.

She nodded. "Yep."

"But why? I thought you hated magic."

"I do." She looked at him and her expression became grave. "But I hate my parents' killer even more. I think the mystic may be able to help us find him."

Harvey gave her a slight nod. "I guess that makes sense, in a weird way."

"I'm glad you agree."

"Are you sure you want to do this? I could go myself, you know. Give him a description of the pendant and the attack, ask him if he knows anything. You don't have to do it yourself if you don't want to."

Sariah smiled at him. "That's very sweet of you, but no. I need to do this. Besides, I've heard mystics can read people's minds and stuff." She almost spat out the words. The thought of a magician working their mental tricks on her was the last thing she ever wanted, but if it helped track down her parents' killer, it would be worth it. "If he reads my mind, he'll get a better mental image of the attacker." She'd never actually seen all of her attacker's face, just one tiny glimpse. Hopefully, it would be enough.

Harvey had to admit her reasoning was sound. "Okay, I guess you have a point. I'll be there to support you no matter what."

"I think you've made that abundantly clear. Let's get moving again. Where to big man?" She gave him an overly suggestive wink.

Harvey punched her lightly in the shoulder. "Oh no. I'm not about to go there, even with an invitation."

"Aww," Sariah whined playfully.

Harvey cleared his throat. "Anyway, back to the map." He forcefully pointed at a small group of houses on the map. "We started over here in Chatwick. The mystic's house is pretty much directly west of our village." He pointed at the small house. "We've been traveling due west for a while now, so all we have to do is keep heading that direction, and we'll be fine."

Sariah's cheeks burned. She'd been right all along! She should have known it would be simple. All that show of emotion and humiliation for such a small payoff? Not worth it, but it was too late now.

She wanted to punch him in the gut for being a know-it-all asshat, but instead she simply nodded to him. "Sounds good. West it is." She gave him a toothy smile.

Harvey beamed back at her. "Shall we?" He held his arm out like he was walking her to a formal affair instead of trudging through the woods.

Sariah took one quick look at his arm then back up at him. She made a "humph" noise, turned without accepting it and started marching.

Harvey looked disappointed, but he followed. He didn't want to get left behind, especially not now.

The two kept walking, heading as close to west as they could. They didn't have anything like a compass, so all they had to go off of was the placement of the sun in the sky.

It made for slow going because they needed to stop regularly and wait to make sure they were still headed the right way.

At some point, they ended up taking a decently sized detour around a small stream. The stream had not been on her map, which meant it must be relatively new. They followed the bank until the water was barely ankle-deep and they were able to cross.

Sariah figured the detour cost them a good hour of travel time. Combined with the frequent stops to check their direction, she started to worry they wouldn't make it to the mystic's house before dark, which would mean another night camping out in the forest. The last one hadn't been so bad, but she was still on edge from their close encounter with the howling creature earlier.

Who was she kidding? That hadn't been a close encounter, just two scared children afraid of their own shadow.

She let her line of thinking drop. It wouldn't help her quest any to get down on herself even if she probably deserved it.

Sariah looked up at the sky. The sun was nearing the horizon, meaning it would be dusk soon.

She glanced over at Harvey. He looked as tired as she felt. The two weren't in bad shape. Years of working the mines gave them decent muscle tone, but aerobic exercise like hiking was difficult.

She made up her mind. They would have to find a clearing and stop for the night.

Sariah placed a hand on Harvey's arm to stop him from walking. "I think we should find a safe place to spend the night," she told him.

Harvey saw the weariness in her eyes and nodded. "Yes, I think that's for the best."

Sariah pointed behind her. "There was a small clearing a short way back from here. We should go there and-"

She never got to finish her sentence. A slight rustling noise in the bushes behind them was all the warning they got.

A large, hairy wolf pounced from under the brush, aiming right for Harvey. The beast connected and forced him to the ground.

Gabe sat in his old rocking chair and stoked the fire. It was starting to get dark, and he'd need a good flame to cook his nightly repast.

At his feet, his dog Bear was silently chewing on an old

piece of rawhide. He smiled down at the animal. Bear truly had a life of luxury. The dog never wanted for anything. He was a true companion, and that was worth any price.

Gabe got up and went over to his pantry to pull out vegetables for the night's stew. Almost mindlessly, he got to work chopping them into little bits.

As he worked, he heard a low whine from near the doorway. He glanced over and saw Bear standing next to the door, pawing like mad.

"What's wrong, boy?" he asked. "Is it time for our evening walk already?"

The dog turned his head and whined at his master again, then went back to pawing at the door.

He looked down at his potatoes. Only two left to slice. "We'll leave in just a moment, I promise," he told Bear, but the dog was seemingly inconsolable and would not relent, pawing at the door like they had to leave right away.

Gabe got a little worried. It wasn't like his dog to behave this way. Bear was a very well-mannered dog for the most part. He only got upset around bigger dogs, but there were no other dogs in this area of the forest usually.

He walked over to the animal and started petting its head in a calming, rhythmic motion. "Easy, boy. I'm sure it's just a wolf chasing a rabbit or something."

The dog looked up at him. Staring into the beast's big, pleading eyes like he was, Gabe lost his resolve. "All right, Bear, we'll get started on our walk now."

He gave his potatoes on the counter a last longing look and opened the door.

Bear shot out of the house like a cannon, racing into the trees.

Gabe started running after his dog. "Wait!" he cried. Running off wasn't like Bear, either. Something must have really gotten into him.

He ran for a few more minutes before finally catching up to Bear. The animal was standing over the corpse of a squirrel who had definitely seen better days. Its head was gone, and there was a giant claw mark down its side.

Gabe stood and rubbed his chin. "That's odd," he said aloud. "What kind of predator would leave a kill rotting in the forest like this, half-eaten?"

The hair on his neck stood on edge. He took a closer look at his surroundings. The woods were unusually quiet.

Forests weren't loud places generally, but something was always flying, buzzing, crawling, or prowling about. It wasn't normal for the forest to be completely devoid of noise and movement.

He was trying to put the pieces together when the answer came to him in the form of an ear-splitting howl breaking through the silence.

Instantly, he crouched low to the ground. He put a hand on Bear to keep him steady, too. Whatever could make a noise like that wasn't something you wanted to mess with.

"Maybe we should head back, eh Bear?" he whispered to his dog. But the animal had other ideas. Bear snarled and wrested himself free from his master's control, then bounded in the direction of the noise.

"Bear wait!" he called after the dog, but it was too late. The dog was long gone.

"Damn it all!" Gabe started running after his dog once again, ignoring the low branches that snapped at his exposed legs.

That's when he heard the sound of a girl screaming at the top of her lungs.

His stomach sank. Someone was in trouble, and Bear was headed right into the middle of all of it.

Gabe picked up the pace and headed toward the scream. "Hang on, Bear! I'm coming!"

The wolf howled. The sound was so loud Sariah had to put her hands over her ears.

She watched the beast raise one of its massive paws and batter Harvey's body. It appeared to be clawing at his leather tunic as if it was trying to peel it off to reach the soft skin underneath.

Sariah shrieked. Her friend was pinned to the ground by a massive beast as big as she was.

She froze, uncertain of what to do. She heard Harvey let out a yelp in pain as one of the beast's claws found purchase on her friend's now-exposed torso.

The sound was enough to break her out of her haze. She shook off her fear and remembered the knife at her waist, suddenly glad she'd had the forethought to take it out of her pack earlier.

She grabbed the blade and approached the wolf from behind. She had to act quickly but also carefully, lest the beast get the better of her, too.

Sariah waited a second until she could find a proper opening, then lashed out with her knife, plunging it into one of the wolf's joints on its hind leg.

The blade made a sickening noise as it sunk into the

wolf's knee, severing muscle and spurting blood everywhere. Some got in her eye, making her back off while she wiped it away. The beast let out a howl of pain and moved off her friend, its attention diverted.

The wolf stared into Sariah's eyes as a low growl erupted from its lips. It flashed its fangs at her and snarled. The scene was enough to make her legs practically give way.

She had been lucky enough when the beast was distracted, but she wasn't sure she could pull off the same move now.

The beast lunged for her and she dove to the ground, trying to maneuver under the thing. It almost worked. The beast missed her chest, but its good hind leg smashed into her head.

Sariah stayed on the ground. There were stars in her eyes, and her head was pounding from the impact. She could barely focus on the giant creature trying to eat her.

The wolf, on the other hand, seemed to be having no such problem and was licking its chops.

It lunged at her again, but this time Harvey was at the ready. He jumped in front of her, both knives in front of him like a shield.

One of Harvey's blades managed to hit the wolf in the jaw while the other glanced harmlessly off the creature's shoulder.

Both Harvey and the creature tumbled to the ground. Once again, the wolf had the upper hand.

Sariah scrambled up to her knees and readied her blade. She wasn't ready to give up yet.

The wolf looked at her with pain and anger in its wild

eyes. She and Harvey had both given the thing a decent wound, but it was still going strong.

She tried to advance, but the beast was far too fast and dodged out of the way, and she ended up falling face-first into the dirt and brush.

The beast lunged at her and this time, connected with her side. She cried out as one of its massive claws sunk into her previously injured shoulder.

Sariah screamed in pain and despair. Both her and Harvey were on the ground, broken and bleeding, while the wolf was barely injured. Limping perhaps, but only just. The beast had proved too much for them.

The creature snarled at them and reared up on its back haunches, getting ready to unleash a strike that would end them.

Suddenly it stopped and backed down. Then it crouched on the ground and placed a giant paw over its mouth, letting out a low whine like it was in pain.

Finally, the beast turned tail and started walking away. Before long, it broke into a full run, and a moment later, it was gone from view.

Sariah couldn't believe it. They had been saved. Whether by skill or dumb luck, she couldn't be certain, but she was overjoyed.

She felt the sharp pain from the wolf's attack more acutely, and she was dizzy. She looked at Harvey, who was a little bloody. His tunic was probably mangled beyond repair, but otherwise, he looked no worse for the wear.

Gingerly, she reached a hand out to him but couldn't manage to reach far. She tried to stand, but her legs refused to obey her.

Sariah desperately wanted to move away and get her and Harvey out of the wolf's hunting grounds to an area of relative safety, but her body wouldn't listen.

She rolled over onto her back and lay there, waiting for sleep to come and hoped Harvey would be able to pull first watch.

Out of the corner of her eye, she saw a glimpse of a man moving about. She'd never seen him before. He seemed to be shouting at something, but she couldn't tell who or what.

Her last coherent thought was she hoped the man wasn't there to rob them. Then everything went black.

CHAPTER FIVE

Sariah woke up several hours later to an unfamiliar sensation. Her upper left arm was in intense pain, and if she didn't know better, something was licking her hand.

Was it the wolf playing with his meal before devouring it? No, it couldn't be. She sensed no malice or evil from the bizarre perpetrator, and somehow knew she was no longer in immediate danger.

Her eyes fluttered and eventually opened. She glanced in the direction of the odd sensation. A big, furry dog with bright eyes beamed back at her. The animal saw her waking, yelped once, and backed off.

She stared at the panting creature before her in amazement. Just where was she, and how did she get here in one piece?

Sariah shot up into a sitting position and took in her surroundings. It was dark, but she could make out the big details. She was in bed in a small room in a house. The walls looked old and worn but also unfamiliar. There was a small table and chair in one corner of the room, but the space was otherwise devoid of any identifying or personal marks.

At her feet lay her pack, seemingly untouched. She glanced at her body and was relieved to find her clothes were still on. There were a couple fresh bandages on her left arm where the wolf had attacked her, but otherwise she appeared to be in good shape.

She heard the door to the room scrape open. She gathered the blanket around her like a shield with one hand and sat up straighter. With her other hand, she reached for the knife at her belt, but it was missing.

"I'm glad to see you're finally awake," a voice boomed from the slit of the open doorway. The voice was male and foreign but soothing at the same time.

"Who are you?" Sariah demanded.

The door opened the rest of the way, and a man stepped through. Even in the dim light, Sariah could tell he was handsome and well put-together. He had dirty blonde hair and striking blue eyes that pierced through the low light. She guessed he was in his late twenties.

The mystery figure put both of his hands up in surrender. "I mean you no harm, I promise."

His tone seemed genuine, but Sariah still scoffed. Words were easy to come by. She assaulted him with more questions.

"Where am I? Why did you bring me here? What did you do with Harvey? And you still haven't told me your name."

The mystery man took a half step backward. "Easy, now. You're still injured. Let's take things a bit slower, shall we?"

Sariah's eyes narrowed. "I'm still waiting."

The man let out a sigh. "You're right. Where are my manners, anyway? You'll have to forgive me, I very rarely get visitors these days. Especially the unwilling type."

He flashed her a toothy grin. She could see all of his teeth. They looked remarkably perfect and uniform, which was odd. He was trying to gain favor, but it didn't faze her. She crossed her arms over her chest and glared at him.

"Right," mystery man repeated. "Let's start at the top. My name is Gabriel, though I prefer to go by Gabe. I'm a hermit, and I live out here in the Alpenwood alone with my dog, Bear."

At the sound of his name, the dog barked and looked up at his master. Gabe lowered one of his hands and gave Bear a scratch behind his ears, which the animal thoroughly enjoyed.

The tension in Sariah's frame eased as she watched the two. Surely, if the dog liked him, he couldn't be all bad. Dogs were generally a good judge of character, and he hadn't assaulted her as far as she could tell. Her clothes were still intact, and she didn't have any injuries that weren't the fault of the wolf. She supposed she could give him the benefit of the doubt.

"Nice to meet you Gabe," she said at last. "My name is Sariah."

Gabe took a couple more steps into the room and extended a hand in greeting, but she didn't accept it.

"It's nice to meet you, too, Sariah." He lowered his hand back to his side slowly like he was hurt, but Sariah didn't care.

"You still haven't gotten to my other questions."

Gabe looked at her. "Right. That." He maneuvered over to the chair in the corner of the room. "Do you mind if I sit? It's been a busy night." Sariah nodded but didn't take her eyes off him.

"Fantastic. Now, where to start."

He took a deep breath and started to relate his tale about Bear interrupting his dinner plans to run off in chase of a wolf terrorizing the area. When he finally caught up to Bear and the wolf, he saw Sariah and her friend cornered and chased the wolf off, then carried both of them back to his house one at a time.

Sariah bobbed her head a couple of times while he spoke, but she wasn't listening too carefully. Something about it seemed off to her, and she was worried about Harvey. She hadn't seen any sign of him yet.

She gave Gabe a critical look. "If you brought my friend back here, where is he? Can I go see him?"

Gabe smacked himself in the forehead with one palm. "Oh, of course! That's why you're worried."

"What do you mean?"

"I was wondering why you seemed so off-put by the tale, but now it makes perfect sense." He stood up and motioned toward the open door with one of his hands. "Right this way, please. He's in the main room."

Sariah wondered for a moment how he could have possibly known her mood. Something about it didn't seem natural. In fact, nothing about the man who called himself Gabriel seemed natural.

Maybe he's really good at reading people, she thought. It was probably something else, something much darker like magic. The thought made her shudder.

Sariah had heard mystics could read other people's thoughts and moods, among other things. Some of them even did it without thinking, according to her late father. Besides, only someone with that kind of unnatural ability could have scared off the wolf.

She didn't budge. Instead, she cocked her head and confronted him. "You use magic, don't you." It was more a statement than a question.

Gabriel looked confused for a second. "You could say that, yes. I'm what the people of your town refer to as a 'mystic' though the title is disingenuous. True mystics only train in mental magic arts. I'm...not quite that limited."

"Ah hah! I knew it." She wagged an accusatory finger at him. "That was how you took out the wolf!"

Gabe burst into laughter. "That? That wasn't magic. Well, not really."

He fumbled around in one of the pockets in his pants for a second, produced a small, shiny object and threw it to her.

Sariah inspected the object. It was a small metal tube. It looked like a musical instrument with holes for breathing and making noise, though on a much smaller scale.

She tried to look unimpressed. "Am I supposed to know what this is?"

"It's a wolf whistle." He flashed her another smile. "It makes a very unpleasant sound only animals like wolves and dogs can hear. I'm afraid your assailant is still very much alive and well, though he probably won't come around here again for a while."

Sariah looked doubtful. "How do I know you're telling the truth?"

"Are you this critical of all your saviors? Besides, I thought you wanted to see your friend."

She opened her mouth to argue with him but shut it again just as quickly. The man had a point. He'd shown her nothing but kindness, and she had no reason to doubt his sincerity. Other than him being a magic user, of course. Plus, she really was worried about Harvey.

Sariah got out of bed. As she stood, the blood rushed from her head, and she felt a bit dizzy. She had no idea how long she'd been in bed, but apparently it had been long enough to affect her. Either that or the blood loss from the wound on her arm was showing its effects.

She took a step and stumbled. Gabe extended a hand to help her, but she waved it off. "I can handle walking by myself," she insisted. She took another step and fared better. "See?"

Gabe shook his head. "If you say so. Come with me."

He stepped out of the room and turned to make sure Sariah followed. She did, albeit slowly. Bear came over and walked in step with her as though he was worried she would fall over.

With great effort, Sariah eventually made it out of the room and into the hallway. A few more steps and she was in the main room of the tiny house. There, in the middle of the room, she saw a makeshift bed next to the fireplace. In the middle of the bed lay her friend.

"Harvey!" she called and rushed to his side. She placed a hand on his chest. He was still breathing, albeit shallowly. Several blood-soaked bandages were wrapped around his chest. He was definitely in worse shape than she was, but he was very much alive.

Sariah turned and looked at Gabe, who was standing close by. "Thank you," she said. "For saving him, that is."

Gabe grinned from ear to ear. "High praise coming from you." She shot him an icy glare. "But it's really Bear you should be thanking. If he hadn't insisted we go out, I never would have found you."

"Well, thank you, Bear." The dog barked at the sound of his name coming from Sariah's lips. He bounded over and she petted him and scratched behind his ears, as Gabriel had done earlier. The big lug melted under her skilled hands and licked her in appreciation.

"I can see he's taken quite a liking to you."

Sariah smiled. "Yes, well he must have good taste in people, then."

She gave Bear one last pat and turned her attention back to Harvey. His face was quite pale. She inspected his chest wounds the best she could, lifting the bandages to get an idea of the extent of the damage. Fortunately, the claw marks didn't look too deep, but she wouldn't be surprised if he had a couple of cracked ribs.

"Will he wake up soon?" She glanced at Gabe. She wasn't sure why she asked him. Maybe the last few days had taken their emotional toll, and she needed some sort of outside reassurance, that was probably it.

Gabe shrugged. "It's hard to say. He lost a lot of blood like you did. I was able to seal the wounds and bandage him up and make him comfortable. The rest is up to him."

"Can you..." She started to ask him another question, then stopped. She had been about to ask if he could use his magic to heal Harvey, but the thought made her sick to her stomach. She couldn't trust magic, even now.

In her mind, she thought back to her father's accident. He'd been working on a special project with a magic-user. It was supposed to be a simple spell, nothing dangerous, but it had blown up in his face quite literally, and he'd lost the lower half of both his legs.

The risks of using magic were too great. She wouldn't ask unless Harvey's life depended on it.

"Healing is beyond my capabilities, I'm afraid, though there are those who can," Gabe replied as if reading her thoughts.

Sariah was about to say something when she heard the sound of coughing behind her. It was Harvey, and he was starting to wake up.

"Harvey!" she cried. She took his head in both of her hands and kissed him on the cheek.

"Easy," Harvey begged, lifting the hand closest to her and caressing her face. "Please."

Sariah blushed. "Sorry." She withdrew her hands and looked away. "You had me worried, is all."

Harvey's lips curled upward into a wry smile. "What? This?" He motioned with his hand to encompass the wounds on his chest. "Practically a flesh wound, I tell you." He coughed again, worse this time. "I've survived worse." Then he winked at her.

"Oh, you big oaf!" She smacked him on the arm with her good hand, and he winced in pain. "You almost died, you know."

He tried to chuckle, but it hurt too much and he stopped halfway through. "Was it really all that bad? The way I remember it, I almost had the wolf down before you stepped in."

Sariah scowled at him. "I'm serious. You really worried me. Don't ever do that again."

Harvey frowned. He coughed once more and placed a hand on her arm. "I'm sorry," he said sincerely. "I was only trying to lighten the mood."

Sariah softened. She laid her head on an unbandaged area of his torso. "No, I'm sorry. I shouldn't have been so hard on you. You did practically die, after all."

Gabe cleared his throat loudly, and both Sariah and Harvey turned to look at him. Sariah had forgotten he was there.

"I prepared food. You two should eat and get some more rest. You both lost a lot of blood out there." He held two steaming bowls of stew in his hands.

Sariah's cheeks burned hot for some reason she couldn't decipher. She stood up, walked over to Gabriel, and took both bowls. "Thank you again. Your kindness is much appreciated."

Gabe averted his eyes. "Eat and rest up. I'd like to get you two up to traveling health as quickly as I can so you can be on your way. I'm not sure where you were headed, but there's a town called Chatwick not two days from here. You can get better quality care there."

Sariah's eyes lit up. "Chatwick? That's our hometown."

Gabe gave her a weak smile. "Great! Rest up, then. We'll see how you're doing tomorrow."

He took a couple steps backward. "Come along, Bear," he called to his dog, but Bear didn't go with him. Instead, he walked over to Sariah and sat next to her.

He scowled Bear. "So that's how it's going to be, huh? Can't believe I got denied by my own dog!"

Sariah smirked at Gabe. "Like I said, he's a great judge of character."

Gabe shook his head and marched out of the room, sulking. When he was gone, Sariah burst out into laughter.

———

Several hours later, Gabriel crept out of his room. He could hear the sounds of snoring coming from the main room and figured it was safe.

When he reached the main room, he saw the man Sariah called Harvey lying in bed. Sariah was next to him, holding one of his hands. At her feet was his dog, curled around her legs.

For a moment, he wanted to wake up Bear and admonish the animal, but he sighed. It wouldn't do any good and would just wake up his houseguests. They'd be gone soon enough anyway.

He took another glance at his two guests. The girl had spunk, for sure. He could admire that. Hell, he'd even have been attracted to it in another life, but it was pretty obvious where her loyalties lay.

There was a reason he lived on his own, and he was in no mood to change that now.

Gabe put a hand on Harvey's head. The kid had a mild fever. Nothing too serious, but it was enough to worry him. If no one did anything, he wouldn't be fit for travel anytime soon, likely not for several days or even a week. Gabe didn't want that, not in the slightest.

He got to work, clearing his mind. Unlike what he'd told Sariah earlier, he could heal wounds in a pinch, like he'd done with his own scrapes on occasion, but he was far from talented.

His former master on the other hand, could heal damn near anything. The man had been obsessed with the way the Etheric energy used to power magic could be transferred from one individual to another.

He'd only denied it because the girl was so dead set against magic users in general.

He wondered why that was. What had magic done to her that was so terrible? There were few enough magic users in the area. Technically anyone could do it, but so few ever did. He didn't want to fight with her about it, he just wanted her gone.

Once his mind was clear, he began pouring energy out of himself and into Harvey. The boy's injuries started to knit themselves back together.

Gabriel stopped when the wounds were still slightly open but less severe. It wouldn't do to heal him completely. That might look suspicious. He was out of energy anyway. Taking one last look at the happy, sleeping couple he went back to bed.

The sun's rays filtered through a nearby window, waking Sariah from her slumber. She stirred and stretched her arms out, then checked on Harvey. He was still asleep, but he looked a lot better this morning. Bear was nowhere to be found. The dog must have run off in the night. No matter. It wasn't her dog, even if he was cute and warm.

Gabe walked into the room a moment later. "Good

morning, sleepy-head. Let's see how your friend is doing, shall we?"

Sariah groaned. Something about this guy and his attitude rubbed her the wrong way. Still, his mind was in the right place.

She nudged Harvey, and he started to wake up. He opened his eyes and stared at her, a big grin on his face. "Good morning to you, too, lovely," he said suggestively.

Sariah shoved him. "Oh, get off it. How are you feeling?"

Harvey looked thoughtful, then sat up and stretched. Remarkably, there was very little pain, and his wounds didn't bother him near as much as before. "Feeling much better, thank you." He gave Sariah one of his trademark dopey grins.

"Great!" Gabe called. "Then you two can be off this morning. It's been grand, really, but I should get back to my studies."

Sariah scoffed at him. That was a little too abrupt, almost suspiciously so. "Wait," she begged. "I still haven't had a chance to properly thank you."

Gabe waved her off. "It's no big deal, really. Anyone would have done it."

She cocked her head to the side. "I sincerely doubt that."

He gave her a slight shrug. "Maybe so. Let's get you two ready to go, shall we?"

Sariah frowned. Gabe was acting far too dodgy. Perhaps she was being too hard on the fellow. It was his life, and she and Harvey were intruders in it. "You're right. I'm sorry."

"No need to apologize." Gabe flashed another smile.

Sariah went to the room she'd occupied earlier and grabbed her pack. She opened it up and looked at the contents. Everything seemed to be in place, including her father's old map.

Fingering the parchment, she remembered why she'd come out here to begin with. Her worry over Harvey had pushed it out of her mind temporarily. She ran back into the main room.

"Actually," she started. "Before we go, there is one thing I was hoping you could do for us."

Gabe jumped as if startled. "And what would that be?"

Sariah's heart was beating fast. She took a deep breath and forced herself to calm down. She only had one chance to phrase this the right way. "Well, you see, I was hoping you could help me out. My parents were murdered recently, and I'm looking for their killer."

Gabe got a shifty look in his eyes and backed away several steps. "You don't think that I..."

Sariah shook her head forcefully. "Good gracious, no!"

"Thank the Patriarch." Gabe breathed a sigh of relief.

"No, I was hoping you might be able to help me identify who the killer was."

Gabe tilted his head to one side. "How am I supposed to do that?"

Sariah's cheeks burned red, and she gave him a flattering smile. "With your magic-y stuff?" She was desperate.

He burst out laughing. "Sorry, kid, but that's not how it works."

"What do you mean?"

Gabe sighed. "Magic can do a lot, but it's not a fix-all. I

can't read everyone's minds and locate random people on a whim."

Sariah's face darkened, but she wasn't ready to give up. She was sure he was holding out. "But I saw-"

Gabe shook his head again. "It doesn't matter what you saw. There are limits to everything. You're going to have to accept this is one of them."

She frowned. Though she wasn't sure what she'd expected, it wasn't that. Trying a different approach, she asked, "What if you came with us, then?"

He gave her a perplexed look.

"You know, helped us out in more mundane ways. You obviously know a lot about the area." She stroked one of his arms gently, which made Harvey blush. "I bet a big, strong man like you would make all the difference in the world." She batted her eyelashes as she spoke. It was a cheap move, but she would do just about anything in her quest for revenge.

Gabe laughed and flashed her a toothy grin. He pushed her hand away. "Nice try, kid, but no. I think I'm good."

"Come on. Please! My father said you were a good man. The kind of guy I could turn to if I ever needed help."

That gave him pause. "Who was your father?"

"My father's name was Marlin."

A vague look of recognition crossed Gabriel's face. His eyes rolled back up into his head as though he remembered something. "I knew a Marlin once. He was a good guy."

Sariah's eyes lit up. "Then you'll reconsider?"

Gabe shook his head again. "Sorry, no can do. I'm not going to help you throw your life away."

She reared back in anger. "What is that supposed to mean?"

Gabe sighed and pulled on his face. "Listen for a second. I'm sure you're brave, and it took some skill to find me out here, but you're not exactly well-equipped for a life and death struggle. Have either of you ever seen real combat?"

Sariah and Harvey glanced at each other, and both shook their heads.

"That's what I thought. Look, whoever did this awful thing to your parents was a bad man, sure, but if they were even halfway trained, they could snuff you out faster than I could snap my fingers." He snapped once for effect.

Sariah's face burned even hotter. "I already took him on once! I held my ground."

Gabe sneered. "You did, did you?" She nodded. "You probably got lucky and caught him unaware when his guard was down. Tell me, honestly, on equal footing, do you think you would have stood a chance?"

She thought back to that fateful night. Her parents' killer had been fast and his weapon sure. With his invisibility trick, he would have been impossible to see coming. She hated to admit it, but Gabriel had a point.

"I guess not," she admitted slowly. She lowered her head.

Gabe shifted and softened his tone. " I'm sure your parents meant the world to you. I believe if anyone could get revenge based on pure attitude, it would be you, but let's face it. You couldn't even face down a simple wolf and live to tell the tale without help."

Sariah's expression became even more dour. He was

right. What was she doing out here? She wasn't a warrior. She had no business chasing after a trained killer. Maybe she should throw in the towel.

"I'm sorry. I shouldn't have even said anything. Harvey and I will leave you alone." Sariah picked her pack up from the ground and walked over to her friend. She offered him a hand to help him stand, which he accepted gratefully.

Harvey tested out both of his legs. To his delight, he seemed to have no trouble standing or moving about.

"Thanks again for everything," Sariah said. "Really, I mean it. We'll let you get back to your life."

Gabe let out a sigh. He wasn't sure why, but he was starting to feel guilty. They were just kids, after all. "Wait. Let me escort you back home. You deserve that much."

Sariah's face lit up again. It was more than she could have hoped for. If he came with her, maybe she'd have more time to convince him to help.

It was a long shot, but desperate times called for desperate measures, and she had precious few options for keeping her quest alive.

She looked up into his eyes. "Do you really mean it?"

Gabriel nodded and sighed again. "I'm probably going to regret it, but yes, I do."

"Yay!" Sariah jumped and gave Gabe a big hug. He started to wonder what on Irth he'd just agreed to.

CHAPTER SIX

Lucien walked through the forests of the Alpenwood at a brisk pace. He glanced behind himself every now and then, even though he knew no one could possibly be following him.

He was still uncertain after his recent meeting with the Master, and he couldn't quite shake his current feeling of paranoia. Why had the Master been so cross with him, he wondered. He hadn't been like that during their previous encounter. Of course, he'd been a lowly student then.

Lucien couldn't shake the sensation something more had changed, and it wasn't just his promotion from student to operative or his partial failure which had brought on the Master's differing mood.

Lucien shook his head in an effort to clear away such thoughts. They served no purpose out here in the forest. All they would do is hold him back and distract him. He was on a mission and was determined to complete it the right way.

He looked up at the sky. The sun was low overhead. In another hour or two, it would duck down below the horizon.

Lucien smiled. The dark was his ally and best friend in the world. He did his best work while it was dark.

He briefly considered waiting for night to fall before going any further, but just as quickly, he discarded the idea.

He had nothing to fear from the light. No one in the small village of Chatwick had seen him the last time he was there. He'd used his magic to make sure of it.

It was a simple enough incantation to make people believe there was nothing there, and it was one that served him well.

He could walk straight through the main gate with his head held high, and his chest puffed out like some noble and no one would be the wiser. There was no need to wait or use his magic. He could save it for later, in case he ended up needing it.

Lucien remembered the girl and shuddered in spite of himself. She'd been a slight thing, yet she'd given him such a hard time. Things would go down differently this time. He was sure of it.

The main gate of Chatwick came into view a few moments later. Two portly soldiers stood guard. They were unkempt, and one of them was staring more at his own feet than the woods beyond the town.

It was obvious from their appearance they were a slovenly lot who had likely never seen any real action. The thought brought a grim smile to Lucien's mind. Things would sure be different for them tonight.

Lucien strode up to the gate guards and gave them a stiff salute. One of the guards returned the gesture. The other kept staring at his shoes.

He walked through the gate triumphantly.

It felt good to know he was pulling one over on the guards. They never once considered him a threat. How wrong they were.

He kept walking. He knew his destination, but he needed to be careful. No one could see him approach the little bitch's house. That would mean witnesses, and there could never be witnesses.

After making several purposeful wrong turns and glancing behind him at least a dozen times to make sure he wasn't followed, he spotted his quarry, the slightly run-down two-story shack.

He approached the front door with a big smile on his face, only to be confronted with the oddest sight. A middle-aged rearick was camped out on the front porch, snoozing away what was left of the evening. A large, crude battle-axe lay at the base of his body.

"Drat!" Lucien frowned. This was a complication he'd never considered. Whoever the rearick was, he obviously cared for the building's former inhabitants.

Not that it mattered to him.

For a moment, Lucien considered slitting the rearick's throat while he slept, but there were still several people in the general vicinity walking about. If any of them caught sight of him or of the body before he could dispose of it, it would spell bad news. Far better to stay quiet and move slowly. Hopefully, he'd be in and out anyway.

He crept up to the house, moving as quietly as he could while trying to act normal. He waited until the area was mostly clear, then reached for the door.

As gently as he could, he pushed on the door handle. It made an awful creaking noise, but then it was done and he was inside with none being the wiser.

He closed the door as gently as he'd opened it, then breathed a sigh of relief. Part one of his mission was complete with no complications.

Lucien looked around the room. There was still enough light to see his way around, if only barely. Which was good, because he didn't want to light anything and make his presence known.

Now all he had to do was find the missing gems and silence the girl and her friends. He rubbed his hands together and got started.

Gabe was doubting whether he should have offered to escort the kids back to town. It had only been two days, but Sariah and Harvey seemed to be doing their best to drive him completely crazy.

At least the trip was nearing its completion. Even at their slower than normal pace, he figured they'd reach the town of Chatwick by nightfall or shortly thereafter.

He looked at Sariah, who was giving him a very studious look. "Do I have something on my face or something?"

Sariah put her finger on her bottom lip. "Sorry. No, not

exactly. I was thinking to myself you're so much younger than my father said you were."

Gabe let out a slight snicker. "Marlin wasn't it? I think I remember meeting the guy once, but it was a few years ago. Wasn't that memorable, though. I'm shocked he even remembered me."

Sariah wrinkled her nose. "Really? He couldn't stop talking about you. He said you helped him out with a couple really sticky situations when he was new to the area."

He thought about it, but nothing was ringing a bell. He'd lived a fairly solitary existence since he'd moved in. A new thought dawned on him.

"Ah, I bet your father was referring to my mentor, Jakob."

"You had a mentor?"

"Of course. Everyone who knows magic has to learn it from someone. I learned from my old mentor. He used to live in the old wood cabin where I currently make my residence. Up until he left, that is. He said it was time for him to 'find something new to work toward,' if I recall correctly."

Sariah smiled. "Yes, Jakob. That sounds vaguely familiar. Was he an older gentleman? Graying hair, with a long beard?"

Gabe nodded. "Yep. So, your father knew him well?"

"Oh, very. Like I said, Jakob was very helpful to my father before his accident. My father used to trade in rares and antiques. Jakob was good at identifying some of the stranger pieces and finding willing buyers to support his trade."

"That sounds like good old Jake, all right." Gabe chuckled.

He flashed Sariah another smile, and she returned it. He marveled at how everything had turned out. A few days ago, he was enjoying some downtime, and now he was babysitting two kids and talking about his old mentor's exploits. Life was funny like that sometimes.

"Do you think we're close to home?" Harvey asked.

Gabe glanced at the young man. He was boisterous and full of energy like his companion, but something about the kid grated on him and set him on edge. What exactly it was, he couldn't be sure. Maybe it was the sound of his voice.

He gave the young man a curt nod and pointed at a line of smoke on the horizon. "Do you see that?" Harvey dipped his head. "That's your hometown. We're getting close."

"Yay!" Harvey replied. "It'll be good to be back."

Sariah had a concerned expression. "Do you suppose Padron is worried about us?"

Harvey nudged her on the arm. "You bet he is! His two best friends in the world up and leaving without so much as saying a word to him? Yeah, I'm sure he's worried sick."

"But he'll forgive us, right? I mean, he has to. Doesn't he?"

"Pfft. He's a rearick. You know how they are. He probably won't even bring it up. Just clap us on the back and invite us out for a drink."

The corners of Sariah's lips edged up in a smile. "Yeah, you're probably right."

"Of course, I am. I'm always right." Harvey gave her one of his big, dopey grins.

Sariah shot Harvey a dirty look and punched him in the side. He winced at the pain. His side still hadn't completely healed from the wolf attack, though it was much better.

The two kept prattling on, but Gabriel tuned them out. He'd listened to more chattering in the last two days than he probably had in his entire lifetime, and that was saying something. Jakob had been quite the talker. Gabe was desperate for peace and quiet. He'd have it soon enough.

He looked down at Bear. The animal walked between him and Sariah as though he couldn't decide who he liked more. With one hand, he reached down and gave the beast a pat on the back. Bear whined at him appreciatively.

Shortly after, Harvey and Sariah fell quiet and the group completed the trip in relative silence, which made Gabe happy.

When they reached the main gate, Harvey ran up to one of the gate guards and gave the man a big hug. "Tim!" he cried. "How have you been, man?"

The guard looked up from his feet and greeted the man with a big, warm embrace. "Harvey! I'm glad you're back." Tim pulled away, and his face turned sour. "Your father has been very worried about you, you know."

Harvey frowned at him. "I know. I'm sorry, I wanted to say something, but this hothead over here almost ran off without me." He grinned and pointed at Sariah.

Sariah's cheeks burned red. "Hey! Who are you calling a hothead?"

Tim and Harvey both snickered in response.

Gabe watched the three exchange more pleasantries. It was good to see his charges were now safe and sound. It meant he could finally make his exit.

He cleared his throat as loud as he could, breaking up the happy reunion. All three turned to look at him. "Well, it's been great meeting all of you, really it has, but I should really get going," he told them.

Sariah gave him a pouting look. "Right now? But it'll be dark soon, and it's not safe after dark. Surely you can stay the night and leave in the morning?"

Gabe shook his head. "Thanks, but no. I've slept in the forest dozens of times. I'll be fine. I really should be getting back."

Sariah tilted her head to the side. "To what, exactly? You never did tell us what it is you do out there all alone."

Gabe shifted his eyes about. "Studies," he blurted out. "I must get back to my studies."

"It's okay, Sariah," Harvey interrupted, placing a hand on her arm. "The man has done more than enough for us. We should let him go."

Sariah scowled at Harvey, then looked at Gabe again with the same pouting look from before. "At least let me make you a meal. You fed us when you didn't have to. The least I can do for you is return the favor."

Gabriel mulled it over. As if in response, his stomach growled. Now that he thought about it, he realized they hadn't stopped for a meal all day. Still, he was ready to be going.

"I appreciate the offer. Really, I do, but I should get going."

Sariah frowned. "Okay, then. If you must."

His dog Bear was sitting next to Sariah and Harvey, grinning and panting like a fool. "Come on, Bear," he called. "Let's go back home."

Bear barked at him and inched closer to Sariah in defiance.

Gabe snarled at his dog. This was twice now the mangy mutt had snubbed him. He wasn't sure how much more betrayal he could take.

Sariah looked down at the dog and grinned. She gave him a good, long scratch behind the ears and told him he was a good boy.

"Come on," Sariah insisted. "Even Bear wants to stay for a meal. I promise you can leave right after."

Gabe let out an audible groan, but he knew when to give up. This battle was lost, and the deciding vote had been cast by his dog's empty stomach. After the last few days, he should have guessed it would end like this.

"Fine. But I am not staying the night." He walked to where Sariah, Harvey, and Bear were standing and motioned for Sariah to guide them. "Lead the way."

***

Lucien grumbled. He was trying to be quick about his search, but he couldn't make a lot of noise without fear of waking up the rearick outside the doorway. At least the area he needed to search wasn't that big.

His eyes did another quick scan of his surroundings. There wasn't much in the way of furniture, just an old couch and a small table, and the missing gemstones weren't under either of those.

It occurred to him perhaps the girl had stumbled across the stones and placed them somewhere safe, maybe her parents' room. That would be quick enough to check.

Lucien ascended the stairs as quickly as he could while remaining silent. Eagerly, he pushed open the door to the room. An awful stench assaulted his nostrils, the smell of death and decay. It was a scent he knew quite well, though he'd never much liked it.

A quick scan of the room showed it had remained largely untouched and uncleaned from the night of his attack. No, the gems would not be here.

That left only the bitch girl's room to check. In hindsight, it made sense the jewels would have been dropped there. It was where the bulk of the fighting had occurred in their scuffle.

He bounded back down the stairs, more careless this time, and headed into the girl's room. He took great care to make sure the door closed behind him. He didn't want to get caught with his back turned in case someone came in while he was busy.

Lucien spared a glance out the window to check and see if anyone was outside and to gauge the remaining light level. Fortunately for him, no one was there, though it was starting to get pretty dark. He'd have to move quickly or risk using a light. He had no intention of being in this town overnight if he could avoid it.

The room before him was in shambles. Clothing and sheets covered almost every inch of the floor. He sighed. This place would not be easy to search without making a noise.

With a scowl, he got to work, flinging clothes and sheets out of the way. Then he remembered he was looking for tiny gemstones. It would be all too easy for one of them to get lost in a fold of fabric.

He sighed. He'd have to go through each article individually, shaking it out as he went.

"Scheisse, this night is going to suck," he muttered.

Lucien moved to the far side of the bed and decided to start his search there. It was where he'd fallen when that little girl had gotten the drop on him. A sudden, jarring impact could have easily shaken those stones out of their holding place.

It took him a few minutes of sorting through the little bitch's dirty laundry, but eventually he came across what he was seeking, two small, round sapphires. They were sitting on the ground, staring up at him and glinting from the moon's light.

The corners of his lips turned upward in a big, greedy smile. Eagerly, he snatched up the gemstones and placed them in a small pouch. He tied a string around the opening and double-checked it to make sure the knot was secure before he placed the bag back into a secure pocket in his outfit. He wasn't going to lose them a second time.

Lucien heard the sound of a door creaking, along with multiple voices. He froze. The girl had come home to roost.

Sariah led the way through the streets of Chatwick like she was a tour guide. Along the way, she pointed out anything she could think of that might be of interest to Gabriel.

She was really trying to buy time until she thought up a plan to get him to stick around longer. Gabe had been right about one thing. Neither she nor Harvey had any real experience going after a trained fighter. They needed help, the kind Gabriel could offer if only she could find a way to convince him to give it.

"Over there is the entrance to the Market Square," she said, pointing.

Gabe nodded. "Uh-huh. And where is your house, again? I feel like we've circled the town twice." His eyes darted around like he felt uncomfortable.

Sariah laughed nervously. "Um, we're almost there. Promise." Damn it, I need more time, she thought.

The trio rounded another corner and stumbled across the sleeping form of their friend, Padron, snoring loudly on her front porch by the door.

"Who's that?" Gabe asked.

A broad smile lit up Sariah's face as she took in the sight. "Padron!" she exclaimed, but there was no answer.

Harvey grinned at Padron, then at her. "Do you think we should wake him? Let him know we're here?"

Sariah chuckled and rubbed her chin thoughtfully. "I don't know. He looks so peaceful."

While she was pondering her next action, Bear took matters into his own paws. He went over to the rearick and started licking the poor man's cheeks.

"Bear!" Gabe cried. "Get back here this instant! No licking strangers!"

Harvey laughed. "That dog doesn't seem to listen to you very well. How are you even friends?"

Gabe rolled his eyes. "Sometimes, I honestly don't know the answer to that question."

Padron groaned, then woke with a start and shot up off

the ground. "Who's there!" he yelled, his eyes darting in every direction. He wiped the dog's slobber off his cheeks, then stared at his hand, unsure how the drool had gotten there in the first place.

"Just little old me," Sariah answered.

Padron's whole face brightened. "Sariah!" he cried. He embraced her in his giant hands like she was going to pass right through them if he didn't hold on tight.

The two stayed like that for a moment, then he took a step back and held her face like he hadn't seen her in months.

"I'm glad yer back safe 'n sound, lass. Ye and Harvey both." He nodded at Harvey. "Yer father is gonna be right worried about ya, lad. Ye should go and see 'im as soon as yer able."

The rearick took in the rest of the scene. "And who might you be, eh?" he asked, pointing at Gabe. He gave Sariah an odd glance and a suggestive wink at the same time.

Sariah punched Padron in the shoulder. "It's not like that at all, you perv." Padron grinned. "This is Gabe. He's a mystic who lives a few days from here. He helped Harvey and me out in the woods, and I brought him back to thank him."

The dog gave a loud bark. "And his dog, Bear, of course," she continued. "You already met him."

Padron rubbed his cheek again. "Aye, that I did." He gave Gabe a critical look. "I trust me friends didn't cause too much trouble fer ya? They're always running off causin' mischief around here."

Gabe flashed him a quick smile. "No, sir. Just glad to be of service." He looked at Sariah and shifted his feet. "Now that introductions are complete, can we go inside? I'd like to get back home as soon as I can."

Sariah's cheeks burned red. "Of course! How silly of me. Right this way. Padron, won't you join us? I'm cooking."

Padron grimaced for a brief second, then it was gone. Sariah's cooking was famous, but not because it was good. He didn't want to disappoint his friend, though. "I'd be honored, lass. Plus, it'll give ya a chance to fill me in on the missing details."

She nodded, then moved to the door and flung it open and stepped inside.

"This is your home?" Gabe asked. "It looks nice."

Sariah rolled her eyes. "Gee, thanks." She motioned for everyone to pile in. "Harvey, will you get a fire started for the meal?"

"Yes, ma'am." He gave her a nod and got to work.

Padron sat down on the couch. The poor piece of furniture groaned on the floor. "So, lass. What happened after the funeral? I need to know."

Sariah had been dreading this. She always knew she'd have to come clean when she returned home, though she'd hoped to weave a more fanciful tale than the one she had.

She started taking food out of Harvey's pack and getting it ready. As she did so, she related her story to Padron. She was so involved in her telling she didn't notice the sound of the window in her room creak open, or the front door close miraculously on its own.

Nor did she catch the slight smell of smoke in the air.

It wasn't until Bear started barking frantically and pawing at the door that anyone even realized the house was on fire.

CHAPTER SEVEN

A knot of fear formed in Lucien's chest. He had expected the girl to come home at some point, but he hadn't expected her to bring half the town with her. At least, that's what it sounded like.

He crouched low to the ground, making sure no one could spot him from outside the window and made his way to the door. He placed his face on the ground and looked through the crack in the door to figure out how many people there were.

Lucien made out four sets of boots and one set of paws. Drat, he thought. They have an animal with them. That meant his invisibility trick wouldn't work.

He didn't like his current odds. Four against one? Even with the element of surprise on his side, in that cramped room it would be too dangerous. There was too great a chance he could be the one injured or even killed in place of his quarry.

He needed a different approach if he were to silence them all and make it back to the Master in one piece.

First, he needed to get out unnoticed, which was going to be a trick.

His eyes moved over to the window. That would do nicely. He crept over and started to push it open. It creaked even louder than the front door had, but he pushed on through. With as much noise the group was making, it was unlikely any of them would hear anything.

In a moment, the window was open and his way out secure. He climbed up and out toward the chill dusk air and freedom.

Now he could focus on his original task.

He took a look around to make sure no one had seen him. Climbing out the window of a girl's room would look suspicious to even the most clueless of bystanders. Luckily for him, there was no one around.

This area of the village didn't seem to be very popular, or maybe everyone was avoiding it because he'd recently killed a few people. Either way, it didn't matter. It worked out better for him.

Lucien leaned against the house and rubbed his chin. He needed a good, solid plan where he didn't get hurt.

All at once, it came to him. The house was made out of old, dry wood. It would burn quickly and easily. If he blocked the exits, he could burn them all alive. His eyes shone brightly in the darkness.

Before doing anything else, he readied his mind and cast his invisibility spell. Then, he went around to the front and locked the door. It would hold for a short time, but he needed better.

He roamed around town until he found sturdy-looking

fallen branches not far off. They'd provide good kindling for the fire, and weight to keep the door shut.

A few minutes later, he had everything set up and ready to go. Miraculously, the girl and her little friends hadn't noticed anything yet.

Lucien grinned from ear to ear. The Bitch and Bastard must be smiling on him this night.

He concentrated on the space in front of him and made rubbing motions with his hands, then pulled them apart. A small fireball appeared before him. It was one of the few spells he'd mastered that did more than play tricks on people's brains, and it was a useful one. It would serve him well here.

The fireball flew through the open window, into the wood he'd piled up, and burst into flames immediately. His smile grew even bigger. Combined with the clothes and bedsheets, the house would be burning in no time.

He went from there to the front of the house and summoned another fireball to light up the wood he'd piled there.

Taking two steps back, he surveyed the scene. Both exits from the house would soon be raging infernos. The inhabitants were done for.

Lucien took one last look at the soon-to-be tomb of a shack. There would be no escaping that hell. The Master would be pleased with him.

He spat at the house for good measure, then turned and walked away, paying the building and its inhabitants no more heed, and wondered what his next assignment would be as he started whistling.

Sariah wrinkled her nose, looking like a bunny rabbit as she did so. Something didn't smell quite right.

She wondered if it was her cooking. Being honest with herself, she wasn't the best cook. No one seemed excited when it was her turn to make dinner.

It didn't smell like burned food so much as it did like smoke. A small fire in the fireplace wouldn't be casting enough smoke into the room to cause a smell this bad.

Right then, Bear moved over to the doorway and started pawing at the wood. He let out a series of loud barks and looked expectantly at her and Gabe.

Everyone grew quiet. Gabe furrowed his brow. "Bear? What's wrong, boy?" he asked, heading toward the dog and placing a hand gently on his head. Bear barked a few more times and kept pawing frantically at the door.

"Does your dog need to go pee?" Harvey asked, but it wasn't a real question. Now that the room was quiet, even Harvey seemed to have picked up on the fact something was off.

Sariah walked to the door and looked at Bear with sympathy. The poor animal was obviously troubled about something and wouldn't calm down. She reached out and touched the wood of the door and retracted her hand quickly and shook it several times. The wood was hot to the touch. It had almost burned her. All the pieces suddenly fell into place. Her own personal nightmare had just gotten worse.

"The house is on fire," Sariah said aloud. The words

hurt to say. This house was all she had left, and now it, too, was in peril. "We need to get out."

The others stared at her like she'd grown three heads. Then, they all heard the unmistakable sound of flames. There was no denying it.

An idea popped into her head. "The window!" she called out. "We can escape through the window in my room!"

Sariah sprinted over to her room and flung the door open. Flames whooshed out to greet her, burning high and hot, eating up everything they touched. All she owned was being destroyed in a flash of fire.

Worse, the flames were far too hot to travel across. That route was closed to them.

She closed her door, but it made little difference. The flames had been invigorated by the burst of air and were now licking at her bedroom door. In minutes, the flames would encroach on the main room, too.

"I'll get us out of here," Padron insisted. He got up and hefted his mighty battle-axe. The rearick looked quite pleased with himself he'd brought it in with him.

Padron moved over to the door and started swinging. His first swipe opened a small hole in the wood, and flames jumped into the room, greedily licking at the wood around them.

Sariah shrieked and Harvey squealed like a little girl. Padron hung his head. "There's no escapin' that way, I'm afraid," the rearick told them.

"This can't be happening!" Sariah shouted. "There has to be a way out of here!"

Gabe's eyes shot to the stairwell. A second story exit

was better than no exit at all. "Up the stairs, everyone! Hurry!"

Sariah went up first, with Bear right next to her. Gabe brought up the rear. When they reached the landing, Sariah opened the door to her parents' room cautiously.

Alas, they were greeted with even more flames. The fire from downstairs had eaten through a good portion of the floor.

"No!" Sariah screamed. "No, no, no!"

As she watched the evil flames eat away at her parents' belongings, something inside her mind snapped. Without thinking, she ran into the room, making a beeline for her parents' bed.

Harvey yelped and tried to go after her, but Gabe held the young man back. "It's too dangerous!" Gabe insisted.

She paid them little heed. She had come in with a purpose, and she meant to complete it. Looking around the room, she tried to remember where her mom had put the memento.

It seemed ridiculous to be hunting for a family heirloom in the midst of this danger, but she was determined to find it. Otherwise, she truly would lose everything.

The heat was so intense she felt like her skin would melt, and the smoke crept into her mouth and eyes, making her cough and her eyes water so bad she could barely see. She fought through the terrible sensations and felt around the bed with her hands.

A few moments of searching and she found the small object she'd been looking for. She wrapped her hands around it. It was hot to the touch, so she used a bit of fabric from her shirt to wrap it and keep it safe.

In the same instant, Harvey burst into action. He bit Gabe's arm, making the older man's arm go slack just long enough for him to wrest himself away. Then he leaped into the burning room, calling Sariah's name.

The sound of her name made her gasp and she turned in time to see him crash into the room and fall on the floor. He'd hit a cracked ceiling beam and wasn't moving.

"Scheisse!" she swore. She bounded over the bed and reached out to him, shielding him from the greedy flames with her own body.

She sat guarding him and watching the flames grow higher. The heat was so intense she couldn't even see the opening of her parents' room.

I guess this is it, she thought darkly. Maybe Harvey would be okay. She looked around them. They were on the second floor of a burning building. No, they were both goners.

Shaking her head, she cleared those thoughts from her head. There was hope yet, she just needed to get them out of there.

With a strength she didn't know she had, Sariah lifted Harvey up and stared into his eyes. They were open and he was coherent. That was a good sign.

Her lungs heaved from the smoke, as did Harvey's. She motioned toward the invisible door with her hand. Harvey nodded. He understood.

Sariah bit her lip and put one arm around his broad shoulders, then she pushed forward through the flames, determined not to give in or to stop, no matter what.

Somehow, the fire wasn't as bad as she'd imagined it would be. Though they were dancing higher and higher, they seemed to almost move out of the way for the two of them as they trudged forward.

A moment later, Gabe saw Sariah and Harvey emerge from the inferno, coughing and wheezing from the smoke. Sariah was glowing as she walked, and the flames appeared to be bending themselves to her will. He gasped. Impossible, he thought. Or was it? Maybe there was more to this girl than he thought.

The two looked unharmed, which was a miracle itself. In the girl's hands, she held a small bauble. Undoubtedly some sort of memento or precious heirloom.

Gabe snorted. He could understand why a young girl would go after something like that, but it was still a stupid move. "Can we get out of here now?" he asked them.

Sariah nodded, but Padron shook his head. "And just how do ya think we can do that, lad? We're surrounded."

Gabe looked behind him. The rearick was right. During Sariah's little escapade, the fire from downstairs had erupted and was now taking over the stairwell. There was precious little hope for them.

He had an idea. It was a spell he didn't often use so he wasn't sure it would work, and he'd never tried it with this many people, but it was the only hope they had left.

"Gather in close, everyone," he insisted. "I know what to do."

They looked doubtful but complied. Even Bear listened to him this time.

With everyone hugging him as tightly as he could, he stammered, "Might want to close your eyes for this."

He cleared his mind and gritted his teeth. His eyes burned red as he concentrated. A few seconds later, Gabe and the rest of the group disappeared in a crack of thunder and a puff of smoke.

Moments later, the group emerged on the street, several feet from the burning structure. Sariah let out a gasp and fell to the ground, away from everyone else. Padron and Gabriel stepped back, and Harvey went to her and offered her a hand.

Harvey had the biggest frown on his face she'd ever seen, but she could barely look at it. Her thoughts were obscured by the flames consuming the last few bits of her home, the last thing she'd had to connect her to her parents and her childhood.

In their haste to leave, she'd even forgotten her pack in the main room that held her father's map. The old piece of parchment she'd once reviled and later treasured was surely gone, too, lost to the fire.

All she had left of her parents was the tiny heirloom she'd managed to wrest out of their room before it, too, was destroyed. A small ruby broach in the shape of a rose her father had bought her mother on the day he'd found out she was pregnant with her.

Tears streamed down in earnest as she watched the flames grow higher. Out of the corner of her eye, she could see some of the townsfolk and the gate guards flailing about, running to fetch water to try and snuff out the flames, but it was far too late. The evil fire had already claimed its victory.

Sariah sat on the ground and wept. At some point, she felt more than saw both Harvey and Padron sit next to her and embrace her. Bear came, too, and sat at her feet, gazing at her with great big puppy eyes and a heavy heart. Even he seemed to sense her despair.

She was grateful for the support but unsure of what to do. Everything she'd ever known was gone now, save for her friends. At least fate had not seen fit to take those from her, too.

Her thoughts took a dark turn, then, as they had at her parents' funeral, and she marveled at the pointlessness of it all. Within two weeks, she'd lost her parents and her home, and for what? Making a lucky find at the bottom of an empty mine?

All she had left now was her lust for revenge, for an inkling of justice. If anything, the fire had strengthened her resolve. She no longer had anything to come home to.

Sariah leaned against Harvey and sat in silence for several minutes, her savior temporarily forgotten. Eventually, Sariah got up and went over to him.

"Thank you," she said, putting a hand on Gabe's shoulder. "Thank you for saving me and my friends. Even if I don't understand how you did it."

Gabe flashed her one of his toothy grins. "To be honest, I don't understand it completely myself."

She cocked her head to the side. "What do you mean?"

Gabe cleared his throat. "It was magic, of course. Physical magic has a great many uses, including teleportation.

I've always known, though I'd never tried it before on anyone but myself. I'm just glad it worked."

Sariah smiled weakly at him but inside her emotions were a mess. Magic had saved her? But magic was awful, evil stuff wasn't it? Even if it had been useful once, its downsides outweighed the good.

Finally, she relented. She was alive and she could debate the morality of the method later. Right now, she was far too exhausted. "I guess I'm glad it worked, too."

Gabe shook her on the arm. "You were pretty great back there, too, you know."

Her eyes narrowed. "How so?"

"In the house, I mean. Saving Harvey after he foolishly ran after you. That took a lot of courage."

The scene came flooding back and she shook involuntarily, coughing again. She'd almost forgotten about it already. "Yeah, I guess so. I don't know, I saw him sitting there with the flames rising all around him and freaked. I got him out of there as quickly as I could. I'm just glad the fire wasn't as bad as it looked."

Gabriel looked at her sideways and gave her a smirk. "It was more than that. You might not have realized it, but that was magic. You used magic to push the flames away from you."

Sariah scoffed at him. Her? Not in a million years. She'd never been trained in its use, and everyone knew you needed a proper trainer to use magic. Besides, she hated the stuff. Surely you couldn't use something you hated.

"I don't think so." She shook her head.

Gabe was firm. "No, really. Trust me. If there's one thing I know, it's magic."

The evil word left an awful taste in her mouth, even when someone else used it. "But I can't use magic. I've never even been trained in it!"

Gabe laughed. "You'd be surprised."

"So what if it was? A fat lot of good it did anyone. My house is still gone." Sariah looked down at her feet.

Gabe took her head in one of his hands and lifted it until she was looking into his eyes. "Come now, it's not all that bad. You lived."

"Humph." She spun and crossed her arms. It was a petty act, but she felt like being petty. "Not much of a consolation prize."

He put a hand on her shoulder and spun her back around. "Hey!"

Sariah glared at him and stuck out her tongue, then turned again. She wasn't in the mood for whatever he had to say, even if he had saved her.

Gabe brought his lips close to her ear. "I could teach you, you know," he whispered. "If you wanted."

She turned to face him, a look of disgust in her eyes. "Excuse me?" She slapped him on the cheek and went back over to her friends. Harvey and Padron glared at him and comforted their friend. Even Bear turned on him once again.

Gabe rubbed the spot where she'd struck him. "What was that for?"

She gave him a defiant stare. "After everything I've been through tonight and all your refusals to even stick around, you want me to go along with you? That's rich."

He frowned. "I didn't mean it quite like that. Come on, with your potential, you could be a great magician!"

Harvey laughed at him. "Dude, that approach is not going to win her over."

Padron got up and put his arms around her, and Bear nestled up closer to her legs. It was a stalwart shield of flesh and fur standing between her and him.

Sariah smiled at her friends, especially the dog. They made their point quite clear to her. "See? Even Bear agrees you're an idiot."

Gabe frowned at his dog. "You mangy mutt. See if I go out of my way to get you treats again." Bear barked at him once and looked up at Sariah.

"I think it's pretty obvious where his loyalties lie, don't you?" She snickered at him and gave Bear a big pat on the head.

"Come on. I'll go with you on the stupid quest of yours. Just think about it."

That gave Sariah pause. She was enjoying her little power trip. It was fun to be the one with something someone else wanted, even if that something was her.

She decided to let it drop. Loathe as she was to admit it, having Gabe on her side would prove useful. Not to learn magic, of course. He could take his little spellbook or whatever and shove it where the sun don't shine. No, it was his worldly knowledge she could use. That and his sword arm.

She didn't want to seem too eager, either.

Sariah rubbed her chin. "I guess you could come with us if you promise to help. But I don't want anything to do with your magic." The word still felt sour on her lips.

Gabe stood still for a full minute, thinking about the

proposal. She desperately wanted to know what was going on in that head of his.

Finally, he spoke. "I accept your proposal. No magic training. For now, at least, though I bet you'll come around soon enough."

The corners of Sariah's lips curled upward into a creepy smile. Yes, this sense of power felt really good.

"I knew you'd see it my way."

CHAPTER EIGHT

Harvey walked in silence next to Sariah and Gabriel, with Bear in the lead.

It had taken about a day and a half for their group to finally leave Chatwick. Sariah had wanted to leave immediately, but Gabriel had argued against leaving at night, saying daytime travel would be safer. He was right, but it had still taken some convincing.

Then, of course, they needed to figure out supplies and food for the trip. After the fire, nearly all of their supplies had been wiped out, including their tools and even the majority of Gabe's things.

Their next destination, the city of Stratton, was a good week's march out, maybe longer since he and Sariah weren't used to so much walking. Gabe had told them it was the best place nearby to get information on an invisible magic swordsman. Harvey was pretty sure the older man was being sarcastic, but it was also the only major town near Chatwick, so it made sense to head there first.

Fortunately, Padron had stepped up to help them in the

supply department. Their good friend had been happy to make sure they would be well taken care of on their trip, almost too happy. It was odd he seemed to want them gone so quickly.

Harvey wondered if their friend could be hiding something. Harvey shook his head. No, not Padron, he decided. That man was as honest and straightforward as they came. More likely, he figured there was no way to stop Sariah once she had her mind set on something and it was better to help than get in the way.

The thought made him chuckle, and he spared her a quick glance she failed to notice. Sariah was a force of nature, to be sure.

At any rate, Padron and his fellow migrant rearick had set them up pretty well. Even though there was only a handful of rearick in Chatwick, they always had plenty of money to go around when the stakes were high.

Thanks to them, they had two weeks of food provisions, one new set of clothes each, sleeping rolls, and best of all, new weapons they could use including three swords, a couple of knives, and a wooden bow with plenty of arrows. The last one in particular would be very useful if they needed to hunt for meat. Between the new weapons and the old dagger of the assassin's Sariah refused to let go, they were in good shape.

Harvey wasn't sure what it must have cost Padron to get all those goods together, but it couldn't have been cheap. For now, he was just grateful Padron was on his side.

He kept going back to the last words Padron had spoken to him before they left. The first part was plain enough. He'd warned Harvey not to let Sariah come to any harm lest he ended up receiving even more punishment in return.

No, it was the second part that kept him guessing. "Don't ye worry about nothin' round 'ere, I'll make sure everything is taken care of," Padron had said. What was he taking care of? At first, Harvey had assumed it had something to do with fixing up Sariah's burned down house, but even though the rearick were incredible craftsmen, they weren't lumberjacks, and there wasn't enough free wood around to do something like that. Padron must have meant something else.

He shook his head. Worrying about it didn't do him any favors out here in the wilderness. They were about a days' march outside of Chatwick, heading north and a little east. He'd never traveled much outside their hometown, so he was feeling quite lost. Only Gabe knew exactly where they were going, so he was stuck relying on the man's navigation skills. He wasn't sure how much he trusted him.

Harvey gave their guide a sideways glance. Sariah had trusted the man easily enough, and she was typically a pretty good judge of character. That would have to be enough for right now.

They marched in silence for another half hour or so until Harvey finally got bored enough to do something about it. Still uncertain of what to say to his best friend who had lost everything in less than two weeks, he decided to strike up a conversation with Gabe instead. Bear wasn't much of a talker.

He picked up the pace until he was walking next to Gabriel and said, "So, what's this town like, Stratton? I hear it's a big place." That's what the mine foreman always told them. A few times a year, he took small squads up there to peddle the gems and precious metals they unearthed, and upon his return he'd revel in grand tales of the place. Harvey always figured the man was exaggerating, but maybe not.

Gabe nodded. "It is. Bigger than your little mind could imagine, I bet."

Harvey winced at the insult but let it slide. The man was a temporary nuisance at best. Once Sariah had her fill of revenge, he'd be nothing but a distant memory. It was all he could do not to start counting down the days.

He pressed further. "I heard they have a gigantic marketplace where you can buy practically anything imaginable."

Gabe nodded again. "Pretty close."

Well, I'm not going to get too far like this, am I, Harvey thought. He was going to have trouble breaking up the monotony if he couldn't get Gabe to say more than a handful of words. Perhaps a different topic would elicit a better response, one more near and dear to Gabe's heart.

Harvey cleared his throat. "Tell me more about magic. How does it all work, anyway?"

Gabe looked at him like he'd grown a second head and then glanced at Sariah. The girl humphed and stared at the ground. "Not so scared of the big bad 'magic' word like your friend over there, I take it?"

He gave the older man a big grin. "Nope. Honestly, I've always been curious about it. Every now and then a traveler will come through our town who knows magic and claim it can do wondrous things. Of course, there are the not-so-nice spells we've seen recently. I've always been skeptical about its actual limitations."

Gabriel let out a deep sigh. "The truth about magic, kid, is a longer conversation than we really have time for, even on this decently-sized journey."

Harvey growled at being referred to as a kid when he was almost as tall as Gabe. "Try me. I'm sure even my 'little mind' can grasp the basics."

Their guide looked at Sariah again. Clearly, he was more worried about upsetting her than giving a history lesson. Which made sense, Harvey guessed. She was his main area of interest. Sariah said nothing, though, and kept staring at the ground, which Gabe took as consent.

"Very well. How much do you know about magic? What have people told you?"

Harvey shrugged. "Not much. Some people can cast it, and others can't. What type of magic they can learn varies widely as well."

Gabe let out a small laugh and stopped in his tracks. "I knew there was a lot of misinformation going around, but not that much. Suffice it to say, kid, you were lied to."

Harvey furrowed his brow. "How so?"

"To start off, anyone can use magic. Or at least, darn near everyone, and technically anyone can cast any type of spell, too. Some people are more predisposed to one type or another, so not everyone will end up using it the exact same way." Gabe sighed and turned to face Harvey more fully. "Look, are you really interested in this, or are you just trying to kill time?"

Harvey's cheeks burned red. He'd been caught. "Honestly, I was trying to kill time. It's a long walk to Stratton and all."

Gabe shook his head and started walking again, but Harvey grabbed his arm to stop him. "Wait a second!" he yelped.

The older man turned and rolled his eyes. "Yes?"

"What I meant to say was, initially I was just trying to break up the silence. Now I'm honestly curious. Did you really mean what you said? That anyone can cast magic? Even someone like me?"

This time, Gabe burst out laughing, and almost doubled over. "Sure kid, I meant it. Anyone can cast magic. The ability lies within all of us." He sized up Harvey. "Though having said that, I'm not so sure the 'anyone' bit really includes you."

Harvey's eyes darkened and he stood up straighter until he almost towered over Gabe. "Just what is that supposed to mean?" He was starting to get really angry. He'd put up with the insults up until this point out of deference to Sariah, but this was going too far.

Gabe scoffed. "I mean, look at yourself." He rubbed his chin with one hand and eyed him critically. "Not exactly a superstar, are you?"

"Hey!" It was Sariah, and it seemed she'd had enough, too. "Be nicer to my friend here. Remember, you're only here because I let you join us."

Harvey waved her off with a hand. "Thanks for standing up for me, Sariah, but I can handle this oaf here by myself."

Gabe narrowed his eyes. "Oh? How do you plan on doing that?"

Harvey tapped the sword strapped to his side. "The old-fashioned way, of course."

The older man's eyes lit up and his lips curled into a smile. He let his hand rest on his own blade's hilt. "So that's how it's going to be, eh? In that case, I'd be only too happy to teach you a lesson."

Sariah tried to get in between them, but both men waved her off. Harvey looked at her intently. "It's okay, Sariah. I know what I'm doing."

"Pfft. I doubt that" she scowled.

"Don't worry, sweetheart," Gabe chimed in. "I won't hurt your little darling."

She glared at both of them. "Why must your fragile male egos always get in the way of everything?" She tapped her foot as if waiting for an answer, but none came, so she threw her hands up and backed off.

"Fine. If you two want to play with your sticks, I won't stand in the way."

Gabe sighed and shook his head. He couldn't believe Harvey was actually going to fight him. The kid was obviously out of his league. He watched as the younger man pulled out his weapon like an over-eager trainee on his first day of combat training. No form. No finesse. He was half-surprised the little brat hadn't ended up cutting his own hand off.

The kid motioned for Gabe to unsheathe his sword as well and he obliged, moving slowly and cautiously.

"To first blood sound good?" Harvey asked with more confidence than he could possibly have.

Gabe nodded, but inwardly he was laughing. Where had the kid even heard terms like that? The boy was clearly in way over his head, but they were terms he could live with. It meant he could end the fight without anyone getting too hurt. He was certain Sariah wouldn't approve of him offing her little love interest, even if it was deserved, and he wasn't ready to lose a valuable apprentice.

"Wouldn't have it any other way, kid," he sneered.

The two stared into each other's eyes for a solid minute, daring the other to move. "Go ahead," Gabe finally offered. "Make the first move."

Harvey balked. "Like I'd be that foolish. You started all this. You move first."

Gabe shrugged. "I thought you were an idiot, but I never took you for a coward, too."

The incendiary words made his opponent's blood boil. Harvey let out a shout and leaped forward, full of rage, weapon held out in front like the kid was waving a flag around.

Gabriel brought his own weapon up to block and parried the novice attack with ease, though it took more effort than he thought it would. There was an immense amount of power in the kid's swing. Harvey was stronger than he looked.

He flashed the kid a toothy smile and went in for a strike of his own toward Harvey's middle. The younger man flailed wildly and managed to bat Gabe's sword away just in time.

Pressing his advantage, Gabe took a few more tentative

swings, both high and low. Harvey had to back away to keep from getting hit, but he managed to stay away from the blade's sharp edges.

The kid made another attack, coming in with a broad sweep near Gabe's legs that caught him off guard. He barely parried the move in time, and the force of it knocked him backward several inches.

Harvey grinned at Gabriel. "Not such a little kid now, am I?"

Gabe laughed. Harvey was stronger than he looked, but his form was shit. "You have spunk, kid, that's for sure. But you're still quite rough around the edges." He steadied himself and waited for another attack instead of going on the offensive.

Harvey scowled at him. "What's the matter? Afraid of looking bad in front of the girl?"

Gabe let his eyes trail downwards toward Harvey's midsection, then back up. "With the way you handle your blade, I'm not the one who should be worried about what Sariah is thinking."

The implication got under the kid's skin. Harvey let out a guttural cry and came at him with another series of wild blows. Gabe was able to deflect them all, though with each one it got harder to keep the young man at bay.

Gabe felt sweat start to form on his brow. He took a second to wipe away the bead of liquid with his off hand before it could blind him and almost missed a broad swipe at his head.

Ducking to keep the tip of Harvey's blade from giving him a nice new scar, he followed up with a roll around to the back of his opponent and struck out with a back-handed swat using the flat of his blade.

The sound of metal on leather gave off a loud thump as the blow sent Harvey hurtling into the ground.

To the boy's credit, he recovered quickly and never dropped his weapon in the tumble. Gabe gave him a half-smirk. That was a skill not even some seasoned soldiers could muster. Perhaps the boy had promise after all. At least a tiny bit.

He thought about nicking the boy in the back while he was on the ground to end the fight, but he didn't want to hurt the kid's ego too badly. Harvey might complain he was cheating, so he let the kid get back into fighting stance before continuing.

He was about done with this little temper tantrum and was determined to end it quickly before anyone came into any real harm.

Harvey lunged forward with a deep thrust toward his middle section. Gabe saw the blade coming and dodged to the left, moving his own blade in a circle around Harvey's.

When his blade was below his opponent's, he pushed up sharply, forcing Harvey's arm backward, then followed it up with a quick inward swipe of his own. The tip of his blade made contact with the tender skin of the kid's abdomen, cutting through the leather and leaving a small, thin red line not an inch wide behind.

Harvey winced and placed his free hand over the wound while holding up his sword hand in a gesture of surrender. He took steadying breaths and nodded at Gabriel, then sheathed his weapon.

"Good job," the boy said a moment later through

clenched teeth. The older man considered him thoughtfully. He knew what the admission had cost the lad.

Gabe took a second to catch his own breath before returning his own weapon to its scabbard. That little bout had been a better workout than he'd thought it would be.

"I guess I still have a few things left to learn," Harvey admitted slowly. He stuck out his free hand.

Gabe took Harvey's hand in his own and gave it a firm shake. "You weren't half bad back there, either. I was impressed."

Harvey gave him a sheepish grin and raised his shoulders. "Aww, you're just saying that."

"No really, you showed real promise. I mean, you still have a long way to go to even equal a common city guard's skill level, but it's a good start."

The kid beamed at him and gave him a slight bow. "You're very kind, but I know my own limitations. I've never been much with a sword."

Gabriel returned his smile. "Well, that's something we'll have to work on, won't we?"

Sariah stood with her arms folded in front of her and her mouth gaping open, glaring at both of them. "Really?" she balked. "You two practically skewer each other over some nonsense argument and now you're all buddy-buddy?"

The two men both flashed their teeth and looked down at the ground like they'd been admonished by their mother.

Sariah shook her head and walked a short distance away from them. "Men," she muttered under her breath.

Bear stuck his nose in the air and followed after her. It was obvious he disapproved of their antics as well.

"Anyway," Gabe said after a moment's pause. "We should really get back to our mission. We're still quite a way out from Stratton and there's plenty of daylight left to walk by."

Harvey nodded, doing his best to ignore Sariah's continued glares. "Agreed."

Gabriel started moving again. Everyone, including Bear, followed a few paces behind. The four continued in relative silence for about an hour or so before they decided to stop and eat a quick meal.

Harvey dove into the packs and portioned out the food for everyone, then they all sat while they ate and drank deeply. Gabe patted his stomach in contentment and looked up at the sky for a moment. He didn't notice his newfound friend walk over to sit beside him.

"Hey," Harvey called out. Gabe was startled by his voice and jumped.

"What's up?"

"Do you think you could, you know, show me some of those moves you used earlier?"

Gabe looked at the younger man. He had a big, dopey grin on his face and his eyes were lit up with the eagerness of youth. He thought about the prospect long and hard. He didn't really want to take on that kind of apprentice, but he had to admit if the going got tough on Sariah's little suicide mission, it would be good to have extra muscle for back up.

Besides, he thought, maybe I could use this to get on the girl's good side.

"Sure. I'd be only too happy to show you some moves."

Then he raised his voice and stared at Sariah, who was sitting across from them. "You and Sariah both."

Sariah's ears perked up and she looked at the two men. She almost choked on a bit of bread. "Who? Me?"

He nodded in her direction. "Yes, you. You still intend to go after the killer, don't you? How far do you think you're going to get without real-world combat training?"

Sariah's face darkened. It looked like maybe she was blushing but with the shade of the trees, it was hard to tell for sure.

Slowly, she returned his nod. "I suppose you're right. Fine, I'll train with you two. But we only have two swords."

Gabe flashed her his signature grin. "Oh, don't worry. We won't be training with real swords. At least, not for a while. It's far too easy for accidents to happen with real weapons."

It was Harvey who answered him. "When do we start?"

Sariah grunted and pushed back at the oversized branch Harvey brandished at her. They had been training with Gabriel for several hours and the sun was almost ready to duck down behind the mountains.

He'd taught them the basics of swordsmanship, the proper way to grip the handle, how to place your feet for maximum stability. She'd felt pretty foolish standing with a big tree branch in her hands pretending it was a sword, but she could understand why it was necessary.

Gabe had set the two of them against each other so he

could "get a baseline level for their skillset." Harvey had turned out to be quite the opponent.

She'd never fought with him directly before. Her scuffles in the streets of Chatwick had always been with the much rowdier but also much more playful rearick. While they were more than happy to fight a woman, she'd always sensed they were holding back and refusing to go all out.

Sariah stepped back and raised up a hand in temporary surrender. She wiped the sweat away from her face and was breathing heavily. Her arms were extremely sore. Bruises and welts ran up her arms and legs from where Harvey had connected with his branch. The wounds stung, but she bit back the pain and tried to focus on the man in front of her.

At least he's almost as bruised as I am, she thought with a grin. It was a small, petty victory, but she'd take what she could get.

Inwardly, she was starting to feel glad Gabriel was pushing her so hard. The man had been right. She had a long way to go if she wanted to hold her own against her parents' killer. She hated to admit it, but she wasn't as good at this whole fighting thing as she wanted to believe.

As she lifted her branch into the ready position, every ounce of her body ached and screamed in defiance. She raised the branch over her head with the last of her strength and pushed forward with one foot, determined not to be the first to call it quits.

Gabe whistled and motioned for the two to stop.

"That's enough practice for today," he told them.

Sariah let the branch drop and uttered a short prayer of

thanks to the Matriarch under her breath, hoping neither of the two men would hear.

"You both did pretty well today. Better than I would have expected for a couple of young ones from a sheltered country village."

The insult was plain in his tone, but Sariah didn't care. She was far too tired to bother coming up with a witty reply.

She let herself slump to the ground. Bear came up to her and nestled his head under one of her arms. She mindlessly petted the creature with her hand while she struggled to catch her breath.

"Gee, thanks," she said at last. She gave Gabe a sideways glance. "Douche nugget," she added under her breath.

Gabe's eyes widened and he shook his head. She hadn't been quiet enough. "Anyway," he started, "let's break for the night. We're going to need to work double-time if we're going to fit in training sessions and still make it to Stratton before our food runs out."

Sariah groaned. At the moment, all she wanted to do was punch Gabe right in that glib face of his and tell him to go to hell, but she seriously doubted she'd be able to muster up the energy even if she wanted to. Dreams of payback would have to wait for another day.

A tiny portion of her was grateful for his help, even if he was a pompous ass.

She gave Bear another scratch behind his ears, which the dog ate up eagerly, then got some food and set out her bedroll. Gabe graciously offered to take the first watch and let his two "students" get some rest. She wanted to argue and insist she could handle it, but she wasn't sure how she was even still awake, let alone able to stand watch.

Muttering something about how he better not give her special treatment or anything, she drifted off into sleep. She dreamed that night of the wraith that had invaded her home and taken away her safety. His outline kept growing bigger until it engulfed her entire field of view. In the background, she heard a morbid laughter she could only assume came from him.

When Gabe finally woke her just before dawn, she was shaking from equal parts fear and determination. She pulled on her face and rubbed her eyes to finish waking up. As she stood, her aches and bruises from the previous day's battle all came back to her. It hurt to move, but she was determined not to let it get the best of her. She wouldn't show anyone her weaknesses, least of all these two.

The next several days followed in a similar manner. They would march for hours until it got too hot, then they'd take a break to eat and drink before getting into sword practice. Gabe watched her and Harvey fight, stopping them every so often to adjust one or both of their stances or grips and offering pointers for where they could improve their technique.

A couple of times, after a particularly successful bout, he'd let them "reward" themselves by practicing with the bow for a while. The older man set up targets made of sticks and then instructed them on the best way to hold the bow steady and aim it. Sariah took to the bow much quicker than Harvey did, which made her happy. At least she was better at something. It certainly wasn't swordcraft.

After over a week, the trees finally gave way to

sprawling plains that continued out in front of them so far they appeared to never end and shortly afterward, they came across a dirt road. Gabriel explained that some of the bigger cities had cleared out entire paths between them to help trade run smoother. The thought boggled her mind.

Their group walked along the road for some time through the empty plains, then the scenery started to change once again. Farmhouses started to crop up all over the countryside, complete with lush fields of planted crops.

Sariah estimated one of those fields by itself probably had enough grain to feed all of Chatwick for a solid month. She'd never known so much food could exist, let alone all in one place.

The next day, it happened. She was so focused on putting one weary, bruised foot in front of the other she almost missed it.

They reached the top of another rise so much like all the others, and there it was, gleaming like a giant jewel down in the valley, with its back to a massive river. The city below them was massive. It was bigger than she'd ever even imagined in her wildest dreams. So big, in fact, the far side of it was still covered in the haze of the horizon.

Her mouth dropped open and her eyes practically popped out of her head.

Gabe looked over at her and smiled. "Impressive, isn't it?"

She saw him staring and blushed. "I mean, it's bigger than I thought, is all."

The older man snickered. "Say that to all the guys, do you?" He winked at her.

Sariah punched him in the gut and he doubled over. It

felt better than it had any right to, making up for the hell of the last week and a half. "Pervert. I was talking about the city."

Gabe clutched his abdomen and broke out into raucous laughter. Harvey joined in and Sariah's cheeks turned beet red in response.

Gabe stood as straight as he could, a slight chuckle still on his lips. He gave her a grand bow. "Welcome to Stratton, milady."

CHAPTER NINE

Sergeant Ty Genrose looked out at the throngs of people approaching the gates of Stratton. Today was shaping up to be like any other market day. The sun was still early in the sky, but already there was a line of people outside, begging to get into the city.

Most of them traveled with a cart or a large pack of some sort, no doubt hoping they could trade their wares within the city walls for an equally impressive stack of coin.

He sighed as he stopped a couple dragging a small cart behind them and flagged them down to inspect it for contraband. His job was rarely exciting, but that was a good thing. He was too young to remember the Age of Madness personally, but he'd heard the older soldiers tell tales about it. He was glad he'd never had to live in such times.

If the worst thing he had to deal with was sending away the occasional visitor trying to sneak illicit fruit or other substances into the marketplace, it was a good day. So far today, he hadn't even needed to do that.

Ty lifted up the blanket on the couple's cart and inspected the goods underneath. It was a collection of small animal hides, neatly trimmed and already drying. Nothing to see there. He replaced the blanket and motioned for the two to be on about their business.

Another dozen or so carts passed by in a similar manner, each carrying whatever goods the person held of value. He was a little shocked. Usually at least one person tried to sneak in contraband, but today was smooth sailing.

The Sergeant took another glance at the sky. The sun had moved higher up, signaling it would soon be noon, and time for the guards to change shifts. He was glad the day was passing by so smoothly.

He looked out among the throngs and caught something that sparked his interest. Behind another couple of caravans walked a trio of mismatched individuals. They were all armed, which wasn't that odd, but they seemed to have precious few goods or valuables with them.

They were still a ways back so it was hard to make out too many details, but they were quite the sight. The leader of the group was tall and dusty-haired. He was flanked by a brutish teenager with a goofy grin and a slender girl who somehow gave off more confidence than the other two combined. A big, fluffy dog followed at their heels.

Ty wasn't sure why three strange travelers such as themselves would come to Stratton without so much as a bale of hay to barter, but it could only mean one thing. Trouble always followed close behind travelers like them.

As the trio neared his station, he squinted to make out

their faces and was shocked by what he saw. He stood up straighter and tried to look more alert. *What is he doing here?* Ty wondered, referring to Gabriel.

Gabe approached him slowly and stuck out a hand.

The Sergeant took the offered hand in one of his own and looked into the man's eyes. They were bright, but stern.

"Sir," Ty said slowly. "What a pleasure it is to see you here today."

Gabe retracted his hand like it had been bitten and backed up a half-step. There was a look of deep concern on his face. "Pardon?" he replied.

Ty gulped down the lump of fear that had formed in his throat. *Had he said something wrong or offended the man in some way?* "Sorry, sir, we didn't know you were in the area."

Gabe's companions were eyeing him strangely and began backing away. The Sergeant knew he had to do something to diffuse the sticky situation.

Fortunately, Gabe did the job for him. "You must have me confused with someone else," the man offered. "I've never seen you before, and I haven't been to Stratton in years."

Ty blinked a few times. *Was I mistaken?* he wondered. It was rare, but possible. One didn't get to be Sergeant by making mistakes.

"My name's Gabriel." He stuck out his hand in greeting once more. "I'm a humble traveler, and these are my companions, Harvey and Sariah."

The dog behind him barked. "And that there is Bear. Mustn't forget about him. If you ask him, he's the star of the show." The dog barked again, this time in a more satisfied tone.

Ty accepted the hand and shook it vigorously. "Gabriel, you said?" Gabe nodded. He breathed a small sigh of relief. It was not a name he recognized. He guessed it was a case of mistaken identity.

He relaxed his frame and went back to his standard spiel. "And what brings you three travelers here to Stratton today?"

Gabriel chimed in before the others could say anything. "We are but humble travelers seeking food and shelter. We are on a pilgrimage, headed west toward the coast."

The girl with him, Sariah dropped her mouth open and looked like she wanted to argue, but Gabriel silenced her with a wave of his hand and she said nothing. It was a little suspicious, but who was he to argue with a lover's spat. The three looked harmless enough, and they weren't carrying any contraband on them that he could see.

"Good to meet you, Gabriel." Ty withdrew his hand. "The market square should have anything you require. Please be advised your weapons must remain tied in place while you browse the market's wares, and safe travels." He motioned for them to continue on their way.

"Thank you, kind sir," Gabriel replied. Then he took a step forward, leaned in close to the Sergeant's ear, and whispered in a voice so low Ty could barely make it out.

His eyes widened ever so slightly as he took in the information. He opened his mouth as if to say something, but no words came.

All at once, the trio was gone. Sergeant Ty Genrose blinked and wondered if it had all been a dream. He looked out at the remaining throngs of peasants and carts of goods and suddenly felt tired. He called for another guard to take his place and went to go grab lunch. It was early yet, but he figured no one would care.

Sariah punched Gabe in the arm. "What was that for?"

Gabe scowled. "What was what for?"

"You know. Shushing me back there with the gate guard, and that fake story? A pilgrimage? Do we look like a bunch of mystics?"

The older man's face softened and he rubbed his arm. Sariah was really starting to pack a punch. His training must be paying off. "Oh, that."

She gave him her best glare. "Yeah. That."

"You've got to understand. I was trying to get us into the city with as little fuss as possible. What do you think would have happened back there if I'd blabbed to the guard you were coming in here chasing after a serial killer? The guard would have freaked, and rightfully so."

Sariah reared forward on one foot and wagged her finger at him. She opened her mouth like she was going to yell but closed it just as quickly. "I guess you have a point."

Gabe shook his head. That was as close to an apology as he could hope from her, he surmised. He'd take it. "You're damn right I do. Look, I'm sure things are different in your little town in the country, but this is a big place. Three dirty travelers waltzing through the front gate with no goods to sell is going to look suspicious enough as is. We needed a cover story."

Sariah rolled her eyes but finally relented. "Fine. I guess I'll let it go. But next time, you could at least warn us first."

Gabe nodded and breathed a small sigh of relief. He'd thought she was going to bring up the guard's strange reaction to seeing him. For once, he was thrilled to be wrong.

He hung his head low. "You're right, I should have said something to prepare you. I'm not used to traveling with a group."

"Anyway," Harvey interrupted. "What do we do now? Where's the best place to go for information?"

"Easy there, tiger." Gabe pushed the younger man back. "I get you two are desperate and all, but we need to take care of the basics first. We need to secure a place to stay. We can't sleep out underneath the stars. It's not safe to do that in a big city like this. Plus, we need to refill our provisions and find new clothes. We're going to want heavier fabrics in case our quest really does take us out toward the coast."

A light dawned in the younger man's eyes. "Yeah, I guess you have a point. Any ideas on where to stay?"

Gabe rubbed his chin for a moment. "It's been ages since I've been this way. Who knows if any of the places I used to frequent are even still in operation?"

"Well that's not very helpful," Sariah growled.

"There is one place that's probably still in operation. A little outlet called The Dragonfly. We can check it out."

The other two nodded, so Gabriel led the way. They walked through the streets of town mostly in silence interrupted only by the occasional gasp of surprise from one of his two charges. They couldn't believe this many people could possibly congregate together in one spot. It was fun to watch.

After making a wrong turn or two, they arrived at the inn district and came across the place Gabe had mentioned. Even from the outside, they could see the building was in disrepair, with windows practically hanging off their hinges and a door with more dents and scuffs than clean wood, but at least there was light coming from within. That was a good sign.

Harvey and Sariah looked doubtful, but Gabe led them onward. He opened the door and a huge cloud of smoke assaulted their nostrils. The room within was mostly empty and was dimly lit. A thin layer of grime-covered every visible surface. In spite of this, it actually looked pretty inviting.

Gabe walked up to the lone female behind the counter with a big grin on his face. "Evelyn!" he cried.

Evelyn stared back at him with a look equal parts confusion and recognition. Her face warmed and she held out her meaty arms, greeting him with a massive hug. "Gabe! Where have you been all this time?"

He shrugged. "Oh, you know. Here and there."

Evelyn gave him a critical look that said she wanted to press him for more information but held back as she took in his two companions. "And who might these young ones be, eh? Fresh recruits? Seem a bit young for that."

Gabe laughed nervously. "Something like that. They're friends of my old mentor, Jakob. I offered to help them out with a personal matter."

She gave him a wink and a knowing smile. "Ah, I see. I won't press no further, sweetie. Will it be your usual room, then?" As she spoke, she pulled out an old, dusty tome from underneath the counter. Its pages were yellow in several spots, and it looked like the book hadn't been used in weeks. It had the words "Guest List" emblazoned on the front.

"Uh, yeah. Sounds great," Gabe replied. "Listen, I need to talk to my friends in private. Do you mind?"

Evelyn closed the book. "Of course, sweetie. I'll go get the room ready for ya. You don't worry 'bout nothin.'"

The giant woman teetered off up the stairs with remarkable ease and soon Gabe, Sariah, Harvey, and Bear were alone once more.

Sariah was standing in her usual disapproving stance, somehow looking down at him even though her eyes were barely level with his chest. "What was that all about, 'sweetie?'"

Gabe felt heat emanate from his upper body and tugged at the collar of his shirt. "Oh, it was nothing. Just an old friend of my mentor is all."

She didn't look convinced but didn't press the issue, either.

"Anyway," Gabe said, changing the subject. "We still need to find more supplies. We're almost out of food and fresh clothes. Our current attire is looking a little battle-worn, don't you think?"

"And information," Sariah added. "Don't forget the main reason you brought us here."

He nodded. "Right. Three tasks, then, and wouldn't you know it, there's three of us."

Bear snarled and barked a few times. "Four of us, I mean," Gabe corrected himself quickly. "How could I forget you, Bear." He reached out a hand to pet his dog, but the beast snorted and ran to where Sariah was standing.

"Oh come on! I didn't forget you, I swear!" But Bear didn't budge. Once again, he'd lost out to the girl. He threw up his hands in mock surrender while Sariah knelt and scratched the beast behind his ears and called him a good dog. She was getting far too much satisfaction out of it.

Gabe cleared his throat. "As I was saying, we have three tasks to complete before nightfall, so we should split up to complete them faster."

Harvey nodded. "That makes sense. Should we meet up back here, then?"

He grinned. "Exactly what I was thinking."

Sariah whined. "But I'm not even sure how we got here to begin with! This city is massive. How are we supposed to find our way on our own?"

Gabe pointed at his dog. "Bear knows his way around town. He can accompany you two to the market square and back." Bear yelped appreciatively. Hopefully, that meant Gabe was earning points back with the mangy animal.

Harvey chimed in before Sariah could argue further. "I can work with that. Sariah and I will go to the market square, then, while you ask around for information on the killer, and we'll all meet back up here for dinner."

Gabe smiled at him. "Yes, that sounds like an excellent plan." He reached into his shirt pocket and pulled out a few gold coins. He shoved them at Harvey. "Here. This should cover what you need to buy. If you're shrewd about it, at least."

Harvey grinned back at him. "Don't worry, I've bought

plenty of clothes before. I can get us what we need without issue."

Sariah scoffed and punched Harvey in the arm, then wrested two of the coins out of his hand. "I don't think so. She looked him up and down. "I've seen your fashion sense. I think I'll handle the clothes shopping. You can get the other supplies."

Harvey looked wounded. He stole a glance at his own clothes, sniffed once, and looked back at Sariah. "What's that supposed to mean?"

Gabe chuckled and placed a hand on Harvey's shoulder. "Friend, there are some arguments I am not willing to get into the middle of. This would be one of them."

Sariah's face beamed at Gabe's words. She gave the two a smug smile and started heading out the door, Bear following closely at her heels.

Harvey looked down at his leather tunic again and tugged on the front of it. "Come on, it's not that bad, is it?" he whined.

Gabe laughed again. "You better get going if you don't want Sariah to leave you behind."

Harvey turned and saw his friend was already through the door and halfway down the street. "Wait!" he cried. He ran after her, practically stumbling out the door in the process.

Gabe smiled and watched the two leave. Ever since they'd shown up in his life, it hadn't been the same. He wasn't exactly sure where they'd lead him next, but he could count on one thing, it wouldn't be boring.

CHAPTER TEN

Sariah and Harvey walked through the winding streets of Stratton with Bear in the lead. Somehow the furry animal seemed to know exactly how to get to the market square, almost like it had been there many times before.

Maybe he had. Sariah had to admit, she didn't know much about Gabe's history, even though she was putting an awful lot of trust in his guidance. For all she knew, he could be leading them into a trap.

Nah, she reasoned. He hadn't even wanted to come along to begin with. She had practically forced him into it. Not exactly the process of a devious villain.

Her mind made up for the moment, she turned her attention to trying to memorize their path. If the worst happened and they got separated, it'd be good to know how to get back to The Dragonfly on her own.

She looked at Harvey, who was sporting one of his signature goofy grins. It didn't seem like anything ever got him down.

He caught her staring at him and flashed her a toothy

smile. "So, what do you think of this place? Pretty massive, huh?"

Sariah smiled back. "Yeah." She spread her hands out wide. "It's so much bigger than I imagined. How does anyone ever not get lost walking from point A to point B in this place?"

Harvey shrugged. "Dunno. I like it, though."

She cocked her head to the side. "Yeah?"

"Yeah." He nodded. "There's so much to do and look at here. I bet you could work almost any profession in a place like this. No more need to stay stuck in that old mine shaft to make a living."

Sariah let his words sink in. She had been so caught up in her quest for vengeance she'd never really given any thought about what to do when the quest was done. Maybe living in a giant town would be fun. It was hard to say for sure, but it would sure be different.

"I guess you have a point. That is if you don't get lost on the way to work." She winked at him.

Harvey burst out laughing and Sariah quickly joined in. Bear stared at the two like they had gone crazy and waited. Apparently, he didn't find the joke that funny.

"You always know how to lighten the mood," Sariah admitted, lightly shoving Harvey on the arm.

He cradled the pushed appendage for a moment like he was in pain. "Hey, what was that for?"

She looked him in the eyes. "Do I need a reason?"

Harvey rubbed his chin in thoughtful contemplation. "I guess not. Let's get going. I don't want to even imagine how confusing this place will be after dark."

"You have a point."

With that, the two kept walking. Every now and then one or the other would see something interesting, like a beggar playing an instrument for tips or a group of people gathered outside a restaurant squabbling over pastries, but their trip to the market square was largely uneventful.

Finally, the buildings gave way to a large, open area filled with all sorts of tents and even more people than the two had seen previously.

Sariah's jaw dropped as she took in the scene. She'd gone to the market in Chatwick often enough, and she'd expected something similar just bigger, and it was, but somehow it didn't do the market square justice.

She marveled as she took in the sprawling throngs of tents and people, under which it looked like you could buy about anything. Not just raw ingredients and tools, but everything. Even fully finished goods were offered up for sale.

Harvey sidled up to her and nudged her on the shoulder.

She looked at him. "We should all stay close," she said.

He nodded in agreement. "Wouldn't want to get separated in there."

The young man extended an arm and Sariah took it, then, locked together, the two thrust into the crowd and let themselves get carried along through the dizzying maze of tents and people.

Sariah had thought the regular city streets were bad, but this was so much worse. The people pressing in from every side seemed more cramped and dangerous than it really was, and she didn't like the feeling one bit.

It continued on for several minutes before the crowds

started to thin out as they got past the entrance and into a less-visited area of the market square. There were still plenty of merchants, and their goods seemed to be of similar quality, so Sariah couldn't figure out why they weren't as populated as the ones she'd seen.

Undaunted, the two kept going until Harvey spotted a tent filled with all sorts of foodstuffs set not too far from a similar tent filled to the brim with fabrics of every type. There were a couple of stalls in between the two, but not many.

"Looks like this is where we part ways, for a few minutes at least," Harvey told her, pointing toward the food stall.

A sinking feeling settled into Sariah's gut. "I don't know, Harvey. I'd really rather not leave your side all the way back here, even for a little bit."

"Come now, it'll be fine," he insisted with another one of his goofy grins. "We'll only be a few steps away from one another. What's the worst that could happen?"

She still didn't like it, but she was terrible at telling him no. "I guess so. If you're sure."

He smiled broadly. "It's decided, then. See you soon." He let go of her and ducked into the food tent.

Sariah looked down at Bear and took his face in one of her hands and pulled on it until the dog was looking right at her. "Go with him," she said to the beast. "Don't let him out of your sight for one second."

Bear gave her a quiet bark and bounded off after Harvey. Feeling a bit better, she headed to the fabric tent.

She was amazed at both the quality and quantity of the offerings available. She fingered one of the shimmery fabrics near the edge of the tent on her way in. It was soft and smooth to the touch, unlike anything she'd ever felt before.

If the merchant was willing to put such fine material at the edge of the tent, what marvels could possibly await me inside? she wondered.

It didn't take long to find out the answer. Sariah pushed a tent flap out of the way and walked face-first into the most gorgeous dress she'd ever seen sitting on a mannequin. It was covered practically entirely in sequins and lace. She'd thought her mom's wedding dress had been something but compared to this it blew it away.

"Can I help you with something?" an elderly female voice called out from somewhere inside the tent. The owner of the voice approached her. Her hair was white and her skin was cracked and tanned, but she was quite beautiful for someone of her advanced age.

Sariah blushed and tried her best to smooth out the fabric of the dress she'd bungled into. "Uh, nothing, really," she said. "In all honesty, I should probably get going."

She tried to back out of the tent, but the older woman was faster than she and closed the gap between them. She put a hand on Sariah's shoulder.

"Nonsense," the old woman replied. With her other hand, she gently caressed Sariah's road-weary face. "Now, what brought you in here? Looking for clothes, I assume? I assure you, my prices are quite reasonable. Better than most of the merchants you'll find in these parts. I can guarantee that."

Sariah's blush grew deeper. "What makes you say that?"

The older woman backed up a step and looked her up

and down. " I need to ask? Those clothes are practically in tatters. Not that the rest of you looks much better at the moment."

"S-sorry."

The old woman smiled at her. The motion seemed to crack the taut skin on her face. "Come now, there's no need for such talk. I understand. The road here isn't easy. Many who reach Stratton look even worse."

Sariah's body softened. She had to admit she didn't know what she currently looked like. Standing in front of a mirror hadn't been a priority lately. After everything she'd been through in the past two weeks, escaping the fire, the marching, the training in the woods, she could only imagine she must look a complete mess.

Likely didn't smell much better, either. She should be glad the old woman hadn't thrown her out of the tent entirely looking and smelling the way she did.

"I guess you…I mean, yes, I am looking for some clothing," Sariah eked out at last. Each word felt like a battle to get out of her mouth.

The old woman's smile grew broader, cracking her weathered skin even more. She extended a hand in greeting. "The name's Valerie. I'm a humble clothing merchant at your service."

Sariah took the offered hand and shook it gently, afraid she might break the poor woman if she did it any harder. "I'm Sariah. A traveler from Chatwick on a pilgrimage."

Valerie cocked her head to the side. "Mystic?"

Sariah wrinkled her nose in disgust. "Ew. No. I mean, err, no, ma'am, no I'm not."

Valerie let a slight chuckle escape her lips. "Good." She

leaned in closer to Sariah to whisper in her ear. " I've never really liked those magic-y types, you know?"

Finally, here was a person she could relate to, someone she could trust. "Yes, I know exactly what you mean."

"Now tell me, what did you come in for? Looking for a pretty dress to woo a traveling merchant?"

Sariah laughed. "Uh, no. Just some good old-fashioned traveling clothes for my companions and me. Two gentlemen."

Valerie's eyes widened and she snickered under her breath. "Are they now, you cheeky monkey you."

Sariah blushed even harder. She didn't like where that train of thought was going at all. Well, maybe just a little. She shook her head. That line of thinking would get her nowhere.

"It's completely platonic, I assure you," she protested. "They're childhood friends. Well, one of them is at least."

Valerie nodded. "Aye, I understand. But do they? That's always the more pressing question."

She wrinkled her nose. "What is that supposed to mean?"

The older woman waved her off with a hand. "Enough chatter. Let's get you situated and back to your friends. I'm sure they're worried enough about you as it is."

Sariah wasn't sure what Valerie meant exactly, but she agreed. She'd taken enough time bantering. She was on a mission and needed to complete it, preferably before Harvey got into trouble. "Yes, I'm sure they are, too."

Valerie didn't seem to catch what she said. The older woman was rifling through a stack of muted color fabrics, tossing fully sewn garments every which way in the process. "How big are your friends now, dearie? I do mean height-wise."

In spite of herself, Sariah blushed again, thankful this time the older woman wouldn't see it. "Um, they're about six feet tall or so. One of them, the younger one, has really broad shoulders."

Valerie shot up straight. "Mm, sounds delicious. Maybe he can stop by later and I can measure him in person." There was a wicked smile on her lips that belied her true intentions.

"No!" Sariah scoffed. "I mean, uh that won't be necessary. He's tied up with his own thing." The explanation was weak. She didn't want the old woman laying her hands on Harvey. He was far too innocent for someone so...experienced.

It was to protect him she told herself.

Valerie walked over to her, chuckling as she went. "Now don't worry, dearie, I meant no harm by it. Just talk is all."

"Of course." She gave Valerie a weak smile.

The old woman pressed a bundle of fabrics into Sariah's hands. "Here you go, dearie. Two well-sewn shirts and pants for your tall, handsome friends you can't bear to part with."

Sariah nodded and briefly inspected the clothes. Valerie wasn't wrong. The stitching was excellent, and the fabric was nice and heavy without being stifling. She wondered if they were too expensive for her. She only had two gold coins with her. "Thank you. How much is it?"

Valerie shrugged. "One gold sovereign for the whole set."

Sariah's eyes brightened. "Really? Thank you so much!" She shifted the clothes under one arm and started wrestling with her money pouch with the other.

Valerie put a hand on her to stop her. "Now, how about yourself? Or won't you be needing clothes on that meat-parade pilgrimage of yours?"

She blushed again. This woman had a way of getting under her skin. She liked it, even if it made her feel foolish. It reminded her of the way her mom had been. She probably would have said the same kinds of things about her current situation.

"Who me?" Her expression was blank. "Oh, I don't need much. Just something similar in a smaller size will do."

Valerie tsked at her. "Oh no, dearie, you're not getting off that easy. I saw how you were eyeing that dress you practically walked into on the way in. What do you say? Want to try it on?"

Her eyes gravitated to the shimmery red folds of the dress in question then back to the woman in front of her. "That? There's no way I could afford something of that high quality."

"Then it's a good thing no one said anything about buying it, now isn't it?" the older woman insisted. "Come, try it on. You'll be glad you did."

She didn't have to be convinced any further. "Well, okay. Where can I change?"

The older woman shrugged again. "Right here, dearie."

Sariah looked around shifty-eyed. "Here? Like, in the middle of the tent?"

Valerie gestured at the empty space. "Who is going to

come peeping, exactly, with all this nothingness around, anyway?"

The thought made her feel uncomfortable, but she relented. As quickly as she could, she shimmied out of her outer garments while Valerie got the gorgeous red dress off the mannequin.

While the older woman worked, she spied the knife Sariah had tied around her midsection, the assassin's blade. Valerie's eyes narrowed at the sight ever so slightly in a tiny gesture of recognition, then just as quickly, it was gone.

"That's a fancy blade you have there, dearie. You should be glad the gate guards didn't see you bring it in here."

Sariah blushed again. She was doing that a lot today. "Sorry, I didn't realize."

Valerie waved her off. "Ain't nothing. Don't worry your pretty little head about it. Where did you get it if you don't mind my asking?"

Sariah opened her mouth but shut it again quickly. She felt strangely comfortable around the older woman but wasn't sure how much she should divulge. Revenge was a risky enough business as it was.

"It's a long story," she said at last.

The older woman responded with another shrug as she unbuttoned the last button and hefted the dress of its perch. "We've got plenty of time while I fasten this onto you, dearie. Might as well spill."

It was Sariah's turn to shrug. What harm could it do? It wasn't like the old woman could go blabbing to many people. Besides, she seemed to recognize the blade, and

Sariah needed information. Maybe Valerie could be helpful in more ways than one.

"Well, you see, that knife murdered my parents."

Valerie's eyes went wide with shock and she practically dropped the dress. "You don't say?"

Sariah nodded. "Mm-hmm, I do." She started relaying the whole sordid tale, then, starting with her not-so-lucky bizarre find in the mineshaft and ending with her trip up to Stratton to try and find the assassin while Valerie's deft fingers worked to fasten the dress around her.

"I don't suppose you know where I could find the assassin, do you?"

Valerie chuckled. "I do hope you're not this abrupt with all the merchants."

Sariah looked appalled. "By the Matriarch, no!"

"Just checking." The older woman shook her head and looked down. "Unfortunately, no I can't say that I do. If you had a name or a face, maybe I could do something, but as it were…"

"I understand."

Valerie's head snapped back up. "But enough dour talk. Just look at yourself! You look grand!" She pushed a bolt of fabric off a nearby mirror and motioned for Sariah to look.

Sariah obliged. She took in her face first, which was every bit as weary as she thought it would be after the last two weeks. Her normally well-kept hair fell in ragged knots that would take hours to comb out.

None of it mattered. The dress was even more stunning on her than it had been on the mannequin, making her look as regal as a princess. She'd never seen anything better in her whole life.

"It's…"

"Stunning, right dearie?"

Sariah nodded again. "Yes. But I can't possibly afford it. I only have a few coins."

Valerie shrugged again. "Nonsense. Consider it a gift."

Sariah's jaw dropped open and her head reared back. "I couldn't possibly accept it! This must have taken hours for you to put together. Besides, it's so impractical."

Valerie was firm and shook her head vigorously. "I'll have none of it. After that yarn you spun for me, it's the least I can do for a cute little thing like you. If I didn't know better, I'd swear it was made for you."

"I don't know what to say."

"Just say you'll take it. You do have a point, it is a bit much for walking around the dingy streets of the city. You'll need something more practical, too. Here, let me help you out of the dress while I find something more appropriate for street travel."

The two women took turns unbuttoning the dress. Valerie wrapped it up in some sort of paper "so prying eyes won't try to steal it," then the older woman found her a couple of regular outfits she could call her own and pressed them into her hands as well.

She now had so many clothes she worried about whether or not she could even carry them all back with her, but Valerie insisted it would be a piece of cake.

"At least let me pay you for the street clothes," Sariah offered, rummaging around in her coin pouch.

"I won't have none of it, dearie. Your money's no good here," the older woman insisted.

Sariah didn't understand why Valerie was being so nice

to her, but she didn't have any reason to doubt the older woman's sincerity, and she was grateful for the unexpected gift.

With her packages in hand, she made her way over to the foodstuffs stall, but neither Harvey nor Bear were anywhere to be found. When she asked the manager of the stall, he told her the man and his dog had headed out earlier, citing he needed to drop off his goods and he'd be back in a flash.

Sariah scowled. It was just like Harvey to do something stupid like taking off. She hadn't taken that long in the clothing stall, had she? A quick glance at the sky told her she had. The sun was practically over the horizon, where before it had still been near the high point.

She decided to wait another few minutes to see if Harvey showed up, not wanting to miss him and not sure she could find her way back to The Dragonfly by herself. When the hour turned to dusk and he still didn't show, she decided to risk it.

The market square was much quieter than it had been earlier in the day and she was able to make her way back to the city streets without any interruptions. Once she passed by the big fountain near the entrance to the city, she felt confident she could make it the rest of the way.

After several more minutes of walking and only getting turned around twice, she finally found herself at the doorstep of The Dragonfly no worse for the wear.

Sariah rushed through the door as quickly as she could to find Gabe waiting for her within. He had a worried expression on his face. "It's about time you showed up. I was about to come looking for you, and make sure you didn't get lost," he said in an amused tone.

She rolled her eyes. "Yeah, yeah, women and clothes. We all know I made it back fine by myself. No thanks to Bear." She never knew quite why, but Gabriel could make her blood boil just by talking sometimes.

Gabe chuckled and flashed her a toothy grin. "Hey, I wasn't going to say anything, but since you did."

"Speaking of Bear, where is that dog of yours? And where is Harvey?"

He waved her off with a hand. "They're fine. Harvey showed up over an hour ago with a bunch of provisions. Said he was going to go back and get some more before nightfall. I'm sure he'll be along soon."

The same sinking feeling from before came to her again. Her whole body tightened with worry. Harvey had said something similar to the food merchant, but in the time she'd been there, he hadn't shown, and she didn't see him at all on the way back here, either.

Gabe saw the look of worry on her face and stood to walk over to her. "Hey. He's with Bear, remember? That little ball of fur may be more trouble than he's worth sometimes, but he won't let Harvey do anything too stupid. I'm sure they'll both be back here soon enough."

Gabe had a point. Harvey was one thing, but Bear? Bear she could trust. "Yeah, I guess you're right."

He nodded, then motioned with his hand toward the staircase. "Evelyn made up the room earlier. Why don't you take the clothes upstairs and set them down? Maybe soak in a bath or something. By the time you're done, I'm sure Harvey will show."

Part of her wanted to argue further, but the pull of rest and a bath, a real bath, not a dunk in a river, was too great for her weary bones to argue with. She decided to take him up on his offer.

As swiftly as she could, she made her way up the stairs and into the room they would be forced to share for the night. She shut the door and placed the clothing parcels on one of the three beds.

Her eyes briefly scanned the remainder of the small space. In the corner, as promised, was a tub full of steaming hot water. It looked more inviting than it had any right to.

Quickly, she undressed and stepped into the tub. The water soothed her skin and seemed to wipe away both the grime and the welts underneath in the same instant.

In the safety and security of the bath, Sariah finally let her guard down for a moment and let the emotions of the past few weeks wash over her.

Before she knew it, she was crying, sobbing her eyes out as she let herself mourn her parents' passing for the first time since before she'd started her journey.

She let herself languish in her thoughts until the water started to cool, then she got out of the tub and put on a fresh set of clothes. Somehow, in between the bath, the new clothes, and a little downtime, she felt rejuvenated, almost like a new woman.

With her head held high, she strode out of the room. A mouth-watering aroma greeted her from below. It must be supper time, and Evelyn had obviously prepared something amazing from the smell of it. It was going to be a good night.

Sariah bounded down the stairs two at a time, eager to greet her friends and maybe enjoy life, if only for one night.

That hope came crashing down when she reached the bottom of the stairwell and was greeted by a frantic Bear pawing at her and Gabe in the corner, a worried look in his eyes.

Harvey was nowhere to be found.

CHAPTER ELEVEN

"Bear?" Sariah asked. "What's wrong, boy?" She took the dog's head in her hands and held it. The poor animal was shivering and coated in a fine layer of sweat. The beast was panting like crazy. He'd obviously been running pretty hard before he showed up.

"It's Harvey, Sariah. Bear came back here a moment ago, but Harvey wasn't with him."

The sinking feeling came back. Her eyes grew wide in shock. "What do you mean? Surely Bear wouldn't have left him somewhere unless…"

"Unless he had no other choice," Gabe finished for her.

In one swift motion, Sariah shot up and headed for the door. She threw it open without a second thought and went out into the night. Bear followed.

"Wait!" Gabriel cried out, running after her. "The city streets aren't safe at night!"

Sariah was halfway down the alley but she stopped and turned to look at Gabe, still by the doorway. "And?" she demanded, hands on her hips in a defiant pose.

Gabe scoffed, incredulous. "And what? You can't go out by yourself! You'll just get yourself in trouble, too!"

She looked him up and down. "Are you saying a simple city is too dangerous for the likes of you?"

His head reared back, and he waved his hands in denial. "I didn't say that." His eyes got a strange look in them. "Hey! Who said I was going with you, anyway?"

Sariah scowled. "You did, remember? When you promised to come with me on this quest in the first place." She crouched down and rubbed the top of Bear's head. The dog hadn't left her side and he accepted the attention happily. "Besides, I have Bear with me. He'll keep me safe if you're not man enough to do it."

"Like he kept Harvey safe?"

Bear growled at Gabe's words and flashed his fangs at him.

"Ooh, he did not like that one bit. Neither did I. I'm sure Bear did everything he could, didn't you boy?" Sariah fired back. She rubbed the dog's snout and scratched him behind one of his ears. Bear always seemed to like it. "At least he's not sitting there hesitating while our friend is in trouble."

Gabe opened his mouth to argue further but shut it. He knew when he was outnumbered. With a heavy sigh and his head bowed, he walked to Sariah and Bear.

"Lead the way, Bear."

Bear let out three sharp barks and ran off into the night. Sariah and Gabe followed closely on his heels.

The three made their way in the semi-darkness, meeting no resistance. It seemed no one but city guards were out and about at this hour.

Sariah let her thoughts take a darker turn. Maybe Gabe was right. If none of the city denizens were out save for the guardsmen, maybe it really was dangerous after dark.

She couldn't let herself get wrapped in thoughts like that. Harvey was in trouble. Every instinct in her body told her she needed to find him, and that came first, even before her own quest.

What kind of person would she be if she let Harvey suffer or die only so she could exact her revenge a little sooner? What would she have to come back to? Not much, that's for sure. No, she was on the right path.

They followed Bear in silence for several minutes. The animal seemed to be taking them back toward the market square, which made sense, as Harvey had been headed back there the last time anyone had seen him.

When they reached the open area of the market, Bear doubled back, then veered to the left, like he was heading toward the town entrance.

Their current trajectory made no sense. What on earth could Harvey have been doing? Sariah wondered why he would be heading out of town. Her concern for him grew.

Sure enough, Bear took them right past the big fountain and toward the entrance of town where they'd been grilled by the gate guard earlier that day. The doors of the gate were sealed shut.

A pair of guards, no one she recognized from earlier, stood stalwart at the gates, undoubtedly to keep people like her away. Harvey was out there somewhere, though.

Sariah strode up to the guards like she owned the whole city. "Let me pass," she demanded of them in the firmest voice she could muster.

The guard on the left chuckled. "No one is allowed in or out after dark, miss," he countered in a voice completely devoid of emotion.

"Please!" Sariah implored. "My friend is out there somewhere, and he's hurt. I need to get through!" As if to accentuate the point, Bear pawed at the gate furiously, though the guards didn't pay him any attention.

"I'm sorry, miss, but rules are rules," Monotone replied. "And the rules say no one is allowed in or out."

Sariah growled. "You don't understand! He's hurt and he needs me!"

Monotone stepped forward a half-step and lowered his halberd in a vaguely threatening motion. "That may be, but I'm afraid I can't make an exception just because you asked nicely."

Sariah reared back like she was going to punch Monotone in the mouth, but Gabe reached out and held her arm. He dragged her forcefully away from the two guards. "Come on," he said. "There's no use arguing with the likes of them. It won't work."

She wasn't ready to admit defeat, but Gabe had a point. The two heartless no-name gate guards weren't going to budge outside of a real emergency.

She thought maybe she could cause one, but then shook her head. As tempting as it might be to burn down half the town just to get outside and help Harvey, she didn't know where she'd find enough firewood. She'd need a different plan.

"Let's go back to The Dragonfly," Gabe offered, extending a hand. "I'm sure we can come up with a good plan there."

Sariah was about to accept when another thought came to her. Her eyes lit up like a madwoman's. "Hey, I know! You can magic us across!" she suggested loudly.

Gabe ducked his head low and shifted his eyes about. "Quieter please!" he insisted. "What do you mean, exactly?"

"You know like you did back at the burning house. You can use your magic-y thing to send us to the other side of the gate!" She was louder than Gabe liked.

He laughed at her. "No."

Sariah gasped in shock at his staunch refusal. "What do you mean, no? Why not?"

Gabe looked around like a wanted man. "First of all, if you don't quiet down or let us get out of the street where we can discuss this rationally, I'm not doing you any more favors." He shifted his weight backward and crossed his arms. "And it doesn't look like you have many more options."

"Humph!" Sariah scowled in frustration. She shoved him with all her might. He stumbled backward a half step. "Some friend you are!"

"Who said anything about being friends? I'm here to help you on your quest, not wipe your nose every time you sneeze."

"Humph!" But he was right. She had no right to demand he respond like a true friend would. Their relationship wasn't like that, and even though he'd been chummy enough with Harvey on their trip up here after their little spat, she knew where his true interests were.

That didn't mean she had to be nice about it, though. She rolled her eyes at him and shoved him again for good measure, though more playfully this time. "Fine. We can do it your way."

Gabe flashed her a big grin. "I thought you'd see it my way. Shall we?"

Sariah grimaced. "Ugh. Fine." She wagged a finger at him defiantly then started trotting off toward The Dragonfly. While she had little choice but to agree, she didn't have to look happy about it.

Gabe shook his head and followed, calling to Bear to come with them, which the dog reluctantly agreed to. It seemed even Bear was against him once again.

Together, the three made it back to the inn with no real resistance. A few seedy beggars accosted them for coin at one point, and Sariah whined when Gabe didn't give them anything. Having recently become homeless herself she had a soft spot for them, but no one else so much as glanced in their direction.

Once they were back at The Dragonfly and safely within the walls of their room, Gabe breathed a sigh of relief and slumped against one of the beds without any packages on it.

"There," he said aloud. "Now we can talk about all this 'magic-y' stuff in peace."

Sariah was still in a huff. "What's so scary about it that makes you insist we don't talk about it in public, anyway?" She put her hands on her hips in a haughty stance. "You were the one going on about how you wanted to train me in it the whole way up here, and now that my friend's in trouble and needs help, you shy away?"

Gabe took in a deep breath to help steady his voice. This might take some explaining. "Look," he started slowly. "It's one thing to talk about magic when we're in a small town like Chatwick or out in the open, but in a big town like this, it's a different story."

She looked at him expectantly. "Go on."

"Where do I start?" He sat up straighter and smoothed out his clothes while he thought. "Have you ever wondered why there aren't many magicians?"

Sariah got a thoughtful look in her eyes for a moment then shrugged. "Because it's hard?"

That comment made Gabe burst out laughing. "No," he said shaking his head. "No, not really. I mean, it does take time and effort to learn, don't get me wrong, but that has nothing to do with it. No, it's a lack of quality teachers, that's what."

Sariah growled. "Get on with it. We're wasting time chatting."

Gabe nodded and put his hand out in a dismissive motion. "I'm getting right to the point, I swear."

Sariah shot him an icy glare but finally conceded.

"Magic takes time to learn, and a good teacher to help you learn how to access it. Assuming you want to do anything even halfway decent with it, that is."

He pulled on his face. He was dog tired and wanted to get some rest, not prattle on about his sordid history, but it didn't look like Sariah was going to let him get off until he gave her something. If he were to have any shot of training her, like he was hoping, Sariah deserved to hear some of the truth.

"Like I was saying, the reason there aren't a lot of magic users is that you need a good teacher, and the only good teachers aren't very good people for the most part."

The girl scoffed. "You're not a bad person."

This made Gabe chuckled again, a little quieter than before. "You don't know me that well, sweetheart. You might not want to say that just yet."

She cocked her head to the side. "Come on, you can't be that bad. You saved my life twice now. You didn't have to."

Gabriel's face softened. Sariah was paying him a real compliment. He hadn't heard anyone talk about him in that light in longer than he cared to remember.

"I had a different upbringing than most mages. My old mentor Jakob was not your average teacher. He was... different." His eyes got a distracted look in them as he spoke of his old mentor. "But trust me, most magic teachers aren't very good people. They have a certain reputation. So, their students get the same reputation, by default."

A light dawned in Sariah's eyes. "It's a guilt by association thing?"

Gabe nodded.

"We never thought ill of any of the magicians who came through Chatwick." Her face hardened. "Most of the town didn't, at least. I hated them, but I had a reason to."

"Honey, that was Chatwick. Irth could have exploded and that backwater town wouldn't have even noticed."

Sariah gave him glare like she was going to do bad things to him while he slept.

Gabe sighed. "Sorry, but it's true. Small towns like that are largely disconnected from the politics of the outside world. Trust me, it's a good thing. World politics are sketchy."

She thought about it and eventually relented. "Fine. But it's just the two of us now so spill. Why can't you use your magic-y trick to get us past the wall."

"Oh yeah. I'd almost forgotten about that part."

The girl's eyes grew wide and an intense fire burned behind them. "You what? How could you forget about Harvey!"

That had obviously been the wrong thing to say. He had to be more careful when she was angry.

He got up and walked over to her and placed a hand warmly on her shoulder to try and calm her down. "Easy now, I didn't mean it like that. It's just it's late and I'm tired. Long day for everyone, yeah?"

Sariah's frame relaxed, but her eyes retained their fierceness. "I guess you have a point."

"Glad you agree. Anyway, I could have gotten us over the wall, sure, but then what?"

Sariah rolled her eyes. "We rescue Harvey, of course."

Gabe nodded. "Sure, sure. And how do we do that?"

She wasn't about to be deterred. "Follow Bear and track down his captors."

"Uh-huh. How did Bear get out of the gate? It was locked at dusk. If he was still following Harvey's captors, he wouldn't have come back here, now would he?"

Bear let out a sharp bark at his master's mention of his name. It seemed the beast agreed with him for once.

"Bear could track his scent, couldn't you boy?" she

insisted. She reached over and gave Bear a good scratch behind the ears by way of encouragement.

Gabe scoffed. "Look, I love Bear and he's amazing, but he's no bloodhound. He couldn't follow the scent of a steak if I held it in front of his nose."

Bear looked up at his master with angry eyes and huffed, then walked over to Sariah's side. Bear's loyalty had been short-lived.

Sariah rocked forward on her heels and raised a finger, but then dropped it. "Fine. So we can't follow Bear. At least we'd be out there and Harvey would have a chance."

"How often have you been outside a major town like this after dark?" Gabe said in an accusatory tone. "Even your town of Chatwick wasn't safe after dark, was it? It's even worse with a major city like this one. There are thieves and vagabonds to contend with in addition to strange beasts. We'd be sitting ducks without a plan. Especially as tired as we are. No, that path wouldn't get us anywhere."

The girl paused. Weariness was plain on her face as well. "Ugh, fine. You're right. It's just, he'd do the same for me, you know?"

Gabe looked her in the eyes and nodded. "I know."

Sariah took a step backward and turned to face the wall. Gabe thought he saw a hint of a tear in her eyes.

He sighed once more. "Look, we can take up a search in the morning, yeah? I'm not sure how far we'll get, but we can at least look."

"Really?" She turned to look at him again. Her eyes were bright like she had a grand idea. He hated that look, it always meant trouble. "Great! In the morning, we can go after him. You can use your magic-y to track him down, right? Make the search easier."

Yep. Always trouble with this one. Still, it gave him an idea.

"Sorry, it doesn't work quite like that."

Sariah frowned at him. "Well, what good is magic if it can't even help you find your friends when they're in trouble?" She turned to face the wall again and crossed her arms.

This was it. This was his big chance. He went for it. "Well, it can. Sort of. I mean, there's a small chance we could find him with mental magic. Sniff out his location, in a sense, that is."

She turned her head around to face him but left the rest of her body where it was. "I knew it!"

"Here's the thing. That kind of magic, well, it would only really work for people who already shared a bond. You know, had a reason to want to look for each other in the first place."

Sariah turned the rest of the way around. Her face darkened and he could sense she knew what was coming next.

Gabe took another deep breath. Here goes.

"Someone like you. If you used the spell, it might stand a chance of working."

The girl threw up her arms in consternation. "We're back to that, are we?"

Gabe relaxed his jaw. He hadn't realized how tense it had been. "Look, I wouldn't lie to you about this. Magic isn't exactly a fix-all. Sure, you can use it to sense people, to get a feel for their thoughts and where they are in a general sense, but across a big distance, it's not easy. It really would be easier for you to do it. I wouldn't even know where to start. I barely know the kid."

Sariah stared at him intently. Her eyes looked both frantic and exhausted, and at the same time defeated. He couldn't tell whether or not it was a good thing.

His move had been a risky one, to be sure, but he hadn't been lying, either. He really didn't stand a chance of locating Harvey out in the wild by himself.

At last, she relented. "Fine. I'll let you train me tomorrow. But only for Harvey's sake."

Gabe blinked a few times. He couldn't believe it. His plan had actually worked. Once she'd had a taste of the power magic could bring, there was no way she'd want to stop her training, he was sure of it. He'd get his apprentice after all.

The corners of his mouth curled upwards into a broad smile. "Of course, Sariah. I'm only thinking of Harvey."

CHAPTER TWELVE

Sariah groaned. Gabriel was at the side of her bed, shaking her awake. She rubbed the grime out of eyes and opened them fully. Daylight was seeping through the window in their room. She wasn't sure how long she'd been out, but apparently it had been long enough.

Slowly, she sat up and stretched. Mornings had never really been her thing, and even though the bath had helped yesterday, she was still sore from the previous two weeks of travel and weapons training. Plus, she'd slept horribly most of the night.

Her usual dreams about her parents' killer hadn't haunted her, but the replacement dream wasn't any better. She'd dreamt about Harvey being locked away somewhere in a cold cage built of iron, carted away on a wagon. The poor man had been crying out for someone, anyone, to come to his aid, and when he yelled, his captor would reach through the bars and slap him hard across the face to shut him up.

She had no idea whether or not the dream was real, but

it had sure felt that way. After such a terrible night's sleep she was in no desire or condition to be awake at this hour of the morning. Assuming it was morning. It was hard to tell without looking outside.

"Good, you're up," Gabe was telling her as she stretched again, letting out a big yawn at the same time. She rubbed her jaw. She was pretty sure she'd popped something temporarily out of place with that yawn.

Sariah grumbled. "Yeah, I'm up. And?"

Gabe's eyes were bright and cheery. Too cheery. The man wasn't known for his good moods. "And it's time to get started," he beamed.

The previous night's conversation came back to her. Something about magic and training and she'd agreed to be his apprentice to help find Harvey. She moaned. Inwardly, she couldn't believe she'd just folded, but for Harvey, she'd do anything. A friendship like theirs was worth facing down any challenge, even one that made her slightly sick to her stomach.

Even learning magic.

She took in her surroundings once more. Gabe had done his best to clear a big, wide space in the middle of their cramped room. They probably had ten feet cleared in any direction, which was impressive given that the room boasted three beds, a table, and an ornate bathtub.

It was kind of crazy. She was homeless, and yet she'd spent the last night in a room that contained almost as much furniture and riches as her whole house had back in Chatwick, and it was just one room of dozens in a building of hundreds in this giant maze of a town. The scale of it practically made her head spin trying to take it all in. The world was a crazy big place.

In the middle of the room were a couple of smooth, polished stones. A few small ones and a big one probably the size of her closed fist. The clothing and food packages from yesterday had apparently been stuffed underneath the beds because nothing else adorned the room.

She looked at Gabe again. He was surprisingly clean and recently shaven. At least he'd had the decency to put on the new clothes she'd gotten him. Which was a good thing, because he had really been starting to stink.

That thought made her chuckle, and then she thought about how bad Harvey must smell lying trapped in a prison somewhere and that sobered up her mood real fast. She had to stay true today and concentrate on the task at hand to save him. He had to come first.

"What am I looking at," Sariah asked, pointing at the stones.

Gabe flashed her a wide, toothy grin. He was enjoying this far too much. "Get up, I'll show you."

She groaned again but complied. Standing and walking over to him, she said, "Now what, pretty boy?"

Gabe opened his mouth and shut it again in surprise. If she didn't know better, she'd swear he was blushing.

"All right, so I thought back to my first days in magic training, and I've come up with exercises to help you get started." He pointed at the stones on the floor. "We'll be starting with these."

He sat down next to the stones and motioned for her to do the same. She gave him a look like he was crazy but complied. "You have me on the floor. Now what?"

There it was again, a tiny blush in the man's cheeks. She definitely saw it this time.

Gabe cleared his throat. "Anyway…"

Sariah gave him a weak smile. It had taken her a moment, but she finally caught on to her own innuendo, then she blushed as well. "Sorry," she offered. "I didn't mean it like that."

He nodded and patted her on the back. "I know. It's fine."

"About these stones." She picked up the big one. It was completely smooth and cool to the touch. "What am I supposed to do, try to move them with my mind?"

Gabe laughed at her, but she was serious. "No. That's physical magic. A lesson for another day, perhaps."

She cocked her head to the side. "Physical magic?"

He rolled his eyes. "That's right, you weren't listening all those times I talked to Harvey about this on the way up here, were you? You didn't hear me explain the magic fundamentals."

Sariah shook her head. "No, not really. Sorry."

He took in a deep breath and let it out. Some of the cheeriness was gone from his cheeks now. "Okay, let's start at the top, shall we?"

She felt bad now for not listening before. Obviously, she'd hurt his ego. There was a benefit to that, though. He was far too smug.

"Magic comes from another realm known as the Etheric realm. Think of it like a realm full of nothing but wondrous energy. That's a bit of an oversimplification, but it's a starting point. When we use magic, we're accessing this Etheric realm and borrowing its power source for a minute."

She nodded. "Okay, that makes sense."

He continued. "Well, it's not really us, per se. Rather, it's the nanocytes living in our bodies that do it."

"Nanocytes?"

"Think of them like tiny little factory workers who know how to access the Etheric realm and can do our bidding if we know how to ask them properly."

"Kind of like me? A miner hunting for minerals in a mineshaft, except their mine is in a different realm?"

Gabe gave her a big smile. "In a way. Yeah, I guess you could say that. Anyway, these nanocytes as they're called can pull on the power of the Etheric realm in such a way as to grant us magic power, only they also use some of our own energy to do it. We get the energy back eventually, of course, so it's not a permanent loss or anything, but it's a danger to beware of. I've heard tales of people who exploded after using too much magic power."

Sariah grimaced at the thought of exploding. He wanted to teach her how to use this stuff? Maybe she had been wrong to accept his offer. "Got it. Don't use too much power at once. That's a good thing to keep in mind."

"Exactly. Don't worry, you're a natural at this. I'm sure you'll be fine." He flashed her another toothy grin. It was off-putting.

"This magic power manifests in three basic forms of energy that all focus on different parts of us and the world around us. First, there's physical magic. That magic influences our bodies and the world in a very direct way. Calling forth fireballs and moving things with your mind, even people, are examples of physical magic. It's very powerful in its own right, but also very dangerous."

She gave him another nod. "Makes sense. I'll be careful with it."

"Next comes nature magic. As the title suggests, it influences the natural world around us. Think of it like making a pact with plants and animals, convincing them to do what you want. It's almost like bargaining with nature in a sense."

"Bargaining with nature? What, like asking a tree for a hug?" Sariah replied with a chuckle.

Gabe laughed a little, too. "Believe it or not, yes, it's almost exactly like that, but more asking it to grow or swing its branches in a certain way to capture your foe. It can also be very powerful, but it's intensely hard to master."

"Okay, fair enough. We won't start there, I take it?"

Gabe shook his head. "No. Nature magic also lets you heal other people, though, so all the 'tree-hugging' aside, it's got a great many uses. You'll want to pick up some nature magic if you can just for that."

"Healing?" She wrinkled her nose like she was trying to remember something. "That's how Harvey recovered from the wolf attack so quickly!" She shoved him. "You should have told me."

The older man looked downward. "Guilty as charged. You should be thanking me for that. Those injuries would have taken weeks to heal on their own."

"No, it's okay I guess. I mean, it was a nice thing to do and all."

"Let's get back to the history lesson, okay?" Sariah

nodded. "Good. Last of all comes mental magic. As the name might suggest, mental magic doesn't concern itself so much with the physical realm or with nature like the other branches, but with what's inside our heads. It's nowhere near as flashy as the other forms of magic, but it's very powerful in its own right."

He took in another deep breath. "Mental magic has a great many uses. You can read people's thoughts, make them see things that aren't there, or better yet not see things that are."

A flash of recognition passed through Sariah's eyes. "It's true. He was using mental magic when he ⁓"

Gabe nodded and placed a hand on her shoulder. "Yes, I'm afraid so." He looked her in the eyes. A hint of a tear was forming in them. "Do you need a minute?"

Sariah sat up straight and took a few deep breaths. Thinking about the assassin even in this general sense filled her whole body with rage and sadness that made her tense. She was agreeing to use the very weapon he'd wielded so cruelly. What was she doing?

"It's okay," she insisted. "Promise. Continue."

Gabe stared at her for another minute before he started speaking again. "Anyway, mental magic has a great many uses, too many to count. It's also highly undervalued as a rule because it's the hardest of magic to master. One of its uses is particularly important to us today, which is the ability to look into another's mind and feel their feelings, know their thoughts, and yes, even sense where they are."

Sariah gave him a grim nod. "Got it." She pointed to the rock in her lap. "And this? How is this supposed to help me do that?"

"Right. The rock." Gabe stretched out his arms. "You see, I figured this might be a very emotional day for you, and emotions can make it very hard to use magic properly. It's far easier to use magic when you're calm and collected."

She looked expectantly at the rock again and then back at him. "And? I'm not seeing the connection."

"Just look at it. Its edge is perfectly smooth all the way around. Not a single blemish. It doesn't weigh as much as it should. It's almost as light as a feather, and it's calm and soothing in a way. No one expects anything from a rock, right?"

Sariah rolled her eyes. "I guess."

"So that's the lesson this morning. I want you to clear your mind so you can focus. I want you to clear away all your thoughts and become like this rock, still and calm to the core."

She looked at him with a deadpan expression. Then she shoved him so hard he toppled over and almost hit his head on one of the bedposts in the corner.

"What was that for?" he begged.

"Really? A rock? You want me to think like a rock? That's your big revelation?" She threw the rock at him. It bounced off his chest and landed harmlessly in the corner. "I'd be better off flinging these things with my own two hands!"

Gabe got up slowly and dusted himself off. His side hurt from where Sariah had shoved him, but he was no worse for the wear. "Hey! It's important you be calm," he quipped. Then, with his head hung low, he added. "It worked for me."

She felt bad again. He was only trying to teach her, and

she had to admit, she knew nothing about this magic stuff. Maybe he had a point. "Sorry," she said at last.

"It's okay. We need another approach is all. Maybe you can try meditation. Start out by sitting cross-legged on the floor with your hands on your knees, palm up."

Sariah complied. She felt weird getting into the position, but it was freeing in a way, too. It felt good sitting like that.

"Good," Gabe continued. "Now close your eyes and try to focus your thoughts."

She did as he asked, but try as she might, she couldn't stop thinking about Harvey. He was in danger, and she needed to reach him. "I'm sorry, it's no use. Maybe I should just -"

"Wait. Don't give up yet. Focus on something external instead. Something benign."

She opened one eye to glare at him. "Something like a rock?"

He grinned. "Hey, if it works." She rolled her eyes at him. "I got it. Try thinking of a big, golden ball descending on you, covering your whole body with its soft, radiant glow."

She opened both eyes. "I knew it. This whole setup was a ruse to get me to think about your balls."

Both Sariah and Gabriel burst out laughing. They laughed for probably a solid minute before either one could even look at the other directly.

Once the room was calmer, Gabe started talking. "All right, you know what? Maybe calm collected-ness isn't your thing. Maybe we need to start with a more practical application of magic."

"That sounds like a good plan," Sariah admitted.

"Why don't you focus on trying to change the color of your clothes. Make them green instead of white and brown."

"How am I supposed to do that, exactly?"

"With your mind, of course! Remember, you're not actually changing the color of your clothes, you're making yourself, and others, think your clothes are green. It sounds silly, but I promise it's possible."

"If you say so."

To prove his point, Gabe concentrated for a minute. Sariah watched in wonder as his eyes turned bright white, then a moment later his clothes changed with them. All at once he was wearing red clothes from head to toe when they had been beige and brown before. Even his hair had a tinge of red in it all of a sudden.

Her jaw dropped practically to the floor. "How did you?"

Gabe stood up and smiled at her. "See? I told you it was possible." A moment later, his eyes faded color, and with it, his clothes and hair returned to normal.

"You weren't kidding."

"Just try it? You're a newbie. It's okay if it doesn't work right the first time. Maybe start with just the shirt or something."

Gabe started for the door and called to Bear to follow him.

Sariah whined. "Where are you going?"

"I'm going to take Bear on his morning walk. Don't worry, you're perfectly safe here. I'll be back in an hour or two to check on your progress."

Just like that, the man and his dog were out the door and Sariah was all alone with her thoughts and her training.

"Make myself think my clothes are green?" she repeated out loud. "What a lot of hornswoggle this is. How is this supposed to help me find Harvey?"

If she were to have any hope of it, she'd need to manage somehow. She got to concentrating. She thought about her shirt. It was white, or at least mostly white and new. The fabric was soft to the touch. She stared at the material and tried to will it to turn green.

She closed her eyes as forcefully as she could and willed the fabric to be green. You're green, shirt! she thought. She held onto the thought as hard as she could for as long as she could, then opened her eyes.

White fabric, as pristine and new as it had been moments prior, greeted her.

Sariah growled and picked up another rock and threw it at the tub in the corner of the room. It let out a loud clang as it struck the side.

Now I've done it.

She walked over, picked up the rock, and fingered it gingerly. There was a large crack on the side. It was pretty severe. No doubt, Gabriel would be pissed. These were his special rocks, after all. The ones that had helped him with his magic training.

If he found out. Maybe I could use this magic-y stuff to make the rock look whole, she thought. It was worth a shot.

She closed her eyes again and thought about the rock.

Then she giggled because after all the show earlier, here she was, finally thinking about Gabe's damn rocks.

Once her mind was clear again, she focused on the rock, willing it to be whole and not look cracked. She pried open the corner of one eye and looked at the rock with the barest of glances. It was completely unchanged.

Sariah was about to give up, but then remembered she was going about it all wrong. She wasn't trying to make the rock actually whole again, just trying to trick her mind into thinking it was. She didn't need to focus on the rock but on herself and her own mind.

Now that she was on the right track, she closed her eyes and attacked her job with renewed effort. She focused as hard as she could on her own mental image of the rock.

The rock is whole, she chanted in her mind. She kept saying it over again, perhaps a hundred times, as she gently rocked the stone back and forth in her hands, moving one finger over the crack.

Then it happened. She felt more than saw it since she still had her eyes glued shut. The giant crack in the side of the rock was gone.

Furtively, she opened her eyes. There was the rock in her hands, looking every bit as pristine and smooth as it had before. The magic had worked!

"Woohoo!" Sariah hollered, raising her hands in the air and dropping the rock in the process. It fell on her toe and then tumbled onto the ground.

"Ouch!" she cried as she lifted her foot to inspect it. The little rock could be vicious when it wanted to be.

Her foot seemed to be fine, just a little sore, but her concentration was gone. As she picked back up the little stone, she saw the crack had come back. No matter. Now that she knew what she was doing, she could fix it again. But first, she had a task to finish. She needed to make her clothes turn green.

With a broad grin, she smoothed out her clothes, shook out her hands, and got to work.

Gabriel was about finished with his walk with Bear. The two had gone down to the market square to try and get information on Harvey's kidnapping and come back empty. On the way back, he grabbed some fresh pastries for his new student. Bear had also done his business on the way. It felt invigorating to be in a big city like this again.

He smiled as he wondered how long it had been since he'd been somewhere like this. He'd been trapped in that little cabin of his for what felt like years before Sariah had come along. Almost long enough to forget why he'd been out there to begin with. Almost.

He wasn't going to let such thoughts get him down this morning. He had his apprentice now, and even if she was rough around the edges, it was a start. Things would be well soon enough.

The two rounded the bend and started up the stairs of The Dragonfly. All in all, Gabe and Bear had been gone for probably two hours. Plenty of time for Sariah to have made at least a little progress. Maybe changed a splotch of color on her tunic or something.

Anything would be fantastic. He didn't expect much

from a fresh trainee, not even one with as much potential as her.

As he went around the corner and made it to the doorway of the room they shared, he thought how nice it would to be able to spend time with just her and not any other "unwanted baggage."

The term was harsh, perhaps, but even though he had a slight fondness for the kid, he didn't need Harvey around making things more complicated. Plus, it was another body to watch out for, and he was already overtasked as it was.

He sighed. That was mean, he thought. The kid hadn't meant to get kidnapped, he was sure of that, and the boy had spunk. If everything worked out well, he might even be helpful at some point.

Gabe shook his head. He had other things to worry about today. Much happier things. He raised a hand to knock on the door before entering and heard whispers coming from within.

The sound made the hair on his neck stand up. Was Sariah in trouble? Suddenly, he wasn't sure he should have left her by herself like he had. The girl was brash. Who knew what trouble she could get into on her own.

He put one hand on the handle and turned it as quietly as he could. When he was ready, he put all his weight behind the door and shoved it open as hard and fast as he could.

The sight that greeted him was something he never could have prepared for. It was green, and not just Sariah's clothing. Every bit of fabric in the room had turned a sheen of green, from the bed linens to the rug in the center.

Varying shades of it, but still, everything was green as far as he could see.

There in the middle of the room, beaming up at him like a kid who'd just won the big stuffed animal from a carnival game, was his apprentice Sariah, eyes burning bright white.

"Do you like what I've done with the place?" Sariah asked. She waved her arms around in all directions to point at the furniture. "I think I really brightened it up and made it my own."

Gabe's jaw dropped. For a moment, he couldn't think of anything to say. He wasn't sure what he'd expected from a short lesson and a few hours to herself, but it certainly hadn't been this.

Not that he was disappointed. On the contrary, this was beyond anything he'd ever anticipated, and in a good way.

"Sariah, it's...it's -"

"Green?" She was beaming at him like a fool.

Slowly, he nodded and shut the door behind him. "Yeah." His eyes took another few seconds to take it all in. "You outdid yourself."

"Really?"

"Yes, yes you did. Now you can cancel the illusion. You must be tired, and you should save your energy for the next lesson."

"But I liked it green," she whined. Nevertheless, she relented. A moment later, everything was back to the way it was before, and Sariah's eyes dimmed to their normal hazel color.

She started to walk over to him and stumbled, almost

falling to the ground. With his quick reflexes, he reached out and grabbed her before she crashed to the floor.

"I'm sorry," she started. "I guess you're right. This magic-y stuff is more taxing than I thought."

He smiled at the way she called it "magic-y stuff." The phrase had grated on him before, but he was starting to like it the more he got used to her.

"It's okay. You need rest and food. Lots of food." He helped her over to a bed and had her sit.

"Speaking of." He reached into his pocket and pulled out a couple of pastries. "Here you go."

Sariah eyed the pastries greedily like she'd never seen food before. She snatched them and devoured them as quickly as she could.

"Thanks, my savior once again!" she said.

Gabe's grin got even wider. Yes, things were starting to look up quite nicely for him, and from the least likely of all places, a sixteen-year-old girl.

"You eat up and get some rest, and we'll do another lesson this evening," he told her. "Normally, I'd give you a full day's rest, but Harvey's life is on the line. It's best we keep moving through the lessons quickly."

Sariah nodded. "Fair enough," she managed around a bite of a croissant.

"I'll clean up and put the room back together."

"I should really help you out with that," Sariah offered. She started to stand, but he waved her off.

"No, you sit. You need your rest, remember?"

"No, really, I should help you-"

But Gabe wouldn't hear it. He pushed her back down on the bed and got busy picking things up off the floor. In the process, he came across the rock with a giant crack in it.

He furrowed his brow and turned to look at Sariah. "Hey Sariah, what happened to this stone?"

She had a big, sheepish grin and her cheeks were turning a bright red. With a slight giggle, she ducked and hid her face under the blankets.

Gabriel sighed and shook his head.

Women, he thought. Always up to no good.

CHAPTER THIRTEEN

Harvey slowly opened his eyes. His surroundings were dark, but he could make out basic shapes. He looked up at his hands, which were bound with leather ties to a pole in the middle of a tent that had been all he'd known for the past day.

He kept going over the events of the last day, wondering where he'd slipped up. It had been late in the day when he went to make his second trip to the market square, but it had still been daylight. Certainly no one would kidnap someone in the middle of the day.

So he'd thought, and yet here he was, bound and tied to a pole like a common criminal not a days' ride outside town.

The worst part was when his captors took him, no one even batted an eye. He'd cried out for help, screamed as loud as he could, and no one had even stopped to look in his direction.

Are all big towns this cruel, he wondered. It's enough to make me rethink living here, that's for sure.

He chuckled at his own joke and it sent ripples of pain shooting through his side, which was bruised pretty heavily from injuries sustained during his capture.

It was the remnants of another mistake. When he'd been accosted in the alleyway, he'd thought his attacker was alone, but there were two more, just as menacing and dangerous as the first. The third one had smacked him with something blunt and hard right about where his kidney was, which was what had sent him into the ground and made his capture all but a certainty.

Harvey supposed he should have known better. Muggers never attacked alone. Even in Chatwick, where you rarely saw such acts of savagery, a mugger would have been foolish to rush someone by themselves. Of course, muggers didn't usually take prisoners, either.

If he was honest, he had been overconfident about the whole thing. After his combat training over the past two weeks, he felt like he could take on a whole army by himself. He couldn't even manage three ruffians in a city alleyway. Some hero he was turning out to be.

He didn't have long to sit and mellow in his own defeat, for not a moment later someone opened the flap of his tent and walked in. The man was almost as tall as Harvey, and he swaggered quite a bit.

A massive scar covered half of the man's face and he had a missing eye on the right side. His skin was dark and tanned, and it looked like he had a tattoo on his neck.

The oddest thing, though, was the man's clothing. He was wearing what could best be described as an ill-fitting dusty-brown uniform that looked about two sizes too small as if he had stolen it off someone else. If this was the leader of the bandit camp, then why would he need to steal his own clothes?

The one-eyed bandit smiled then and revealed several missing teeth and one gold one. Another oddity to round out his overall bizarre appearance.

"What's your name, kid?" One-eye asked in a gravelly voice that sounded much older than the man looked.

Harvey opened his mouth. His lips were cracked, and his mouth was dry from not having anything to drink in a day, so when he spoke it came out harshly. "H-harvey."

"Got a last name, Harvey?"

For a moment, he wondered if it was safe to tell the truth. "What's it to you?" he said at last.

One-eye grinned even wider and let out a sordid chuckle. Then he back-handed Harvey across the cheek, leaving a fresh scrape. "I'll ask you again."

The pain from the slap was excruciating and Harvey felt something wet and warm pour into his mouth, undoubtedly blood, but he kept his mouth shut and didn't scream like One-eye probably wanted him to.

One-eye looked at him expectantly. Finally, the man raised his fist again.

Harvey shook his head to the side and tried to form more words. "N-no sir," he answered at last. A little of the blood pooling in his mouth dribbled out of the corner while he talked. "I'm a miner from the town of Chatwick on an errand for the town foreman, sir. I promise I don't know anyone here."

"Humph." One-eye spat onto the ground at Harvey's feet. "I don't remember asking for your life story, kid. No one cares who you are. Only what you're worth. Who were you traveling with?"

He tried to think fast. There was no way he was going to tell this man the truth, but he needed a believable story. "I came with a couple other miners to sell some jewels in the big city, sir. But the others have undoubtedly left by now. It was our last day in town yesterday." He hoped the story would be good enough. If no one was there to pay a ransom, maybe they'd let him go.

One-eye shifted the weight between his feet and raised his hand again. "That all?"

Harvey winced in pain and backed away from the hand as best he could. "Y-yes, sir."

"Humph," One-eye said again. Let's hope for your sake those miners care about their friend, then."

The bandit leader turned and walked out of the tent without another glance at Harvey.

Harvey breathed a sigh of relief. At least his story would keep Gabe and Sariah safe, even if it most likely meant his own doom. That was something.

Sariah. His thoughts turned to her. No doubt she had noticed he was gone by now and was frantically looking for him. He wondered what was going through her mind at this exact moment.

"Scheisse!" Sariah swore. She was practicing mental magic with Gabriel again, but this afternoon's tests were not going as easily as the morning's little show had.

Gabe insisted it was okay, that the spell they were

working on now was much harder, and it took most trainees days to even start on it under the best conditions, but she was determined to push herself as hard as she could. Harvey's life depended on it.

Sariah swore again and threw the rock with a crack in it across the room, missing Gabe's head by about an inch. He'd let her keep it, saying it "matched her personality better now." Whatever the hell that was supposed to mean. It had to be some sort of insult, she just knew.

"I'm never going to get the hang of this, you know," she said casually. Patience had never been her strong suit.

"Of course you will," Gabe replied. "You just need to keep trying. It's not easy to read another person's thoughts. You have to practically jump inside their head."

"Jump inside their head? How is that supposed to help me?"

Gabe gave her one of those stupid toothy grins he favored when he didn't know what to say and shrugged. She should have supposed as much. In spite of his claims, he wasn't really that great of a teacher. At least she didn't think so.

He was trying to teach her the mental magic spell for reading another person's thoughts. Or "head-jumping," as he liked to call it since it was more than just mind-reading, and he was having her start with no one other than himself.

Like she really gave a damn what he was thinking about. It was probably something perverted, she thought. He seemed like the type, always shifty-eyed and acting dodgy.

Sariah sighed. "Just go over it again from the start. What I'm supposed to do, that is."

He nodded and went into his spiel. "What you're trying to do is get into another person's head. You're not trying to read my mind, more like you're trying to become a part of it. Almost like a parasite feeding off my brain and experiencing everything I experience alongside with me. It's really euphoric when you actually start to do it."

She grimaced. The mental image of her being a parasite on Gabe's brain was a little much. She shook her head to get rid of it quickly, then a much different thought came to her.

"Wait a second. You haven't…" She pointed an accusing finger at him.

Gabe's face went as pale as a sheet and he reared his head backward. "What? With you? Never!"

She glared at him. "Really. I bet you have at least once. Couldn't help yourself."

He gulped down some air and looked straight at her. "No, never. I promise." He placed a hand over his heart. "I would never violate your trust like that."

Satisfied, she gave him a curt nod. "Good. But with others? Like, maybe Evelyn?"

"You mean our innkeeper?" He chuckled. "I mean, she's nice and all, and pretty easy to mind read honestly, but for the most part no. Once or twice, maybe, but that's it." At that an idea came to him and his eyes brightened. "Hey, maybe you should try her first."

Sariah wrinkled her nose in disgust. "What? With Evelyn?" She shook her head vigorously. "No, thank you. So not my type. I don't want to know what she thinks."

"Oh, but I'm your type?" Gabe fired back with a wry smile.

She shoved him as hard as she could, making him topple over. "I didn't mean it like that, you perv. It looks like I was right about you. A grade-A pervert."

"Hey," Gabe said defensively. "That was uncalled for."

She felt giddy for denting his ego again but said nothing. It was fun getting him all frazzled.

"Let's get back to the training, shall we?"

"Fine." She shot him a sideways glance. "Perv."

In spite of himself, Gabe smiled at the insult, which made Sariah smile back. They sat and looked at each other for a moment before anyone said anything.

Then, looking into his eyes like she was, smiling like an idiot and with both of their guards down, it happened. It was slow at first, but for the briefest of seconds she swore she felt, not saw but felt, him smiling back at her.

There was more there behind the smile. She could sense the smile was just a facade, a mask put on to keep his real emotions at bay. There was darkness beyond it, rattling away inside his head, and some sort of longing. She could feel his longing for something very intently, almost as if she were doing it instead. The object he desired was too hard for her to make out.

The feeling lasted for the briefest of seconds, then it was gone, and she looked away shyly. She felt elated and dirty at the same time like she'd touched on something she shouldn't have.

Kind of freaky, isn't it? a voice boomed inside her head. It was Gabe. He was talking to her, but not with words.

Yeah, it really is, she thought.

Right? Gabe replied inside her head.

Sariah shot him an icy glare. Had he read her thoughts? How dare he. She shoved him again for good measure.

"Congratulations," Gabe said aloud.

Sariah frowned and furrowed her brow. "Do you mean to say I did it? I connected minds?"

He nodded. "For a second, yes. You were inside my head, feeling what I was feeling. Surreal, isn't it?"

Now it was her turn to nod. "Honestly, yeah. But why were you in my head, too? I thought you said you wouldn't do that to me without permission."

"Easy now. I forgot to mention it's a two-way street. When you dig into someone's mind, they get a glimpse of your mind at the same time. If you're not careful about it, that is."

Sariah's cheeks flushed. What had he learned about her in the brief second she wouldn't have wanted him to find out? What fresh intimacy did they now share?

She decided to change the subject. "Why did it break like that?"

"Oh. I put a wall up," Gabe answered honestly. "Sorry, I don't need you messing around in my head too much. I'm a pervert, remember?" he said with another one of those grins.

Sariah chuckled. "Yeah, right." Only the answer was hollow. Even from the tiny bit she'd seen, she knew better now. There was pain and sadness behind those eyes she couldn't comprehend. Considering how much of her own pain she had to tangle with, that was saying something.

She shuddered like she was cold, and Gabe ended up

offering her a coat, which she declined. She wasn't cold so much as confused and still shaken from the experience.

"Is that what it's like every time you connect with someone else's mind?" she asked.

Gabe nodded. "It is, unfortunately. Definitely not something you want to do willy-nilly."

"I can see why."

"Although, if you'll believe it, there's a whole culture out there where everyone gets inside everyone else's head all day long. It's like one big, constant mind share, or so I've heard."

Sariah shuddered again. That sounded maddening. "Really? How do they handle the after-effects?"

Gabe shrugged. "Who knows? Maybe it's not so bad if everyone does it all the time. Maybe they get used to it or something. I don't know for sure, I'm just glad I don't live there. Wouldn't want that kind of life myself."

She smiled at him. "Couldn't agree more. So what's next?"

"Next, you try the same trick, but with Harvey. He's not close by, so it might be quite a bit harder. You'll need to search for him first."

She nodded. It made sense. "Got it. I'll try."

Sariah tried to focus her thoughts on Harvey, but she still felt distracted from her earlier experience with Gabe's mind. They had only been connected for a moment, but she had seen so much. She wasn't sure she wanted to do the same thing with Harvey, and without his permission. But what choice did she have? She had to do something.

Something still nagged at her. "What did you see back

there?" she asked Gabe. "I mean when we connected minds."

Gabe was looking away like he was lost in thought, but Sariah's question snapped him back to reality. "Oh back then? Nothing."

"Nothing? Not a thing?"

He shook his head. "Nope, not a thing. I mean, I could have. I always could. Your mind is easy to read, but then, so are most people. I didn't because I want you to trust me."

"Trust you?" The words sounded foreign on her tongue, somehow, like she shouldn't be saying them.

"Yeah, you know, trust. It's important if I'm going to train you properly."

"Huh," Sariah responded. It made sense, she supposed, but there was more to it, there had to be.

Could it be he liked her? She shook her head and shuddered. No, that wasn't possible. Besides, she wasn't into him. She couldn't be. It must be the whole connected mind thing messing with her brain chemistry.

She looked away from him and noticed her cheeks felt hotter than they should but ignored the thought. There was no time for worrying about such things. She had much more important matters to focus on, like finding Harvey.

With her resolve once more restored, she started searching out with her mind, hoping to find him. Gabriel had told her at the outset of this whole training episode it might not be successful, that even trained mental magicians couldn't always connect with other people over great distances.

It was only because she and Harvey shared a past and a tight bond with one another that there was even a shred of a chance this could work. Even then, it wouldn't work if Harvey's captors had taken him too far outside town, but it was the only hope her friend had.

Sariah latched onto that hope and used it as a lantern to light her way into the darkness beyond their little room in The Dragonfly. She sent that hope outward, flinging it as far away as she could, and thought about Harvey.

She sent out every thought and feeling she'd ever had about her friend. His hair, his eyes, his scent. She thought about how they'd worked together in the mines, trained both in the streets of Chatwick and the forests of the Alpenwood, but nothing made any difference.

No matter how hard she looked and how much of her feelings she put out into the ether, nothing seemed to come of it.

Sariah slumped back against the bedpost behind her. She was exhausted from her search, and from the day's earlier escapades. Gabe was right, and it was a lost cause. Maybe there was no hope for either of them.

Then it struck her. Hope. Hope for the future, in spite of the terrors of the past. The hope they'd impressed upon each other in their darkest days and hours, those hours after the death of their respective parents.

Both of them had lost at least one parent, and they'd been there for each other afterward, comforting each other and acting as a beacon of hope. Maybe that memory would be enough to conjure a connection over any distance.

She thought back to the night when Harvey's mother had died. He'd been practically inconsolable on his parents' floor, almost ready to take his own life. The poor man had been filled with such pain, then, an unimaginable pain she had thought she'd never have to experience.

How wrong she'd been. She knew all about that pain, now, and how terrible it was, and how hard it was to get past. She could connect with him on that pain. She knew it.

She felt Harvey's pain. Only, it wasn't locked away in the distant past, lying on a floor, sobbing like a young babe. It was here and now, playing out intensely across her body.

Physical pain rocked her body as she felt what she could only assume was the force of a powerful blow to her midsection. It was Harvey's pain. She knew it. Someone was punching him. Torturing him in cruel ways, and he wasn't far away.

"West!" Sariah called out as another wave of pain arced over her. "Harvey is west of here!"

She doubled over and almost fell as Gabe raced over to her side. He placed one hand gingerly on her back and took her head in his other hand. "You were successful? You've connected with him?"

Sariah looked up and nodded. "I've seen him. He's alive but hurt. He's in a tent about a half a days' ride west of here."

Gabriel's face turned into a grimace. "You said west?"

She nodded again.

He frowned even harder. "I think I know who has your friend."

Sariah furrowed her brow. Her connection to Harvey had severed and she was fully in control of herself once more. "Who?"

Gabe shook his head. "No time to explain." He held out a hand to help her up. "Come. We must hurry."

CHAPTER FOURTEEN

Harvey opened his eyes. He was still in the tent, alone and hurting. A while back, a guard had come in and given him food and water. The bandits didn't want their victims dying before the ransom could be paid. He'd eaten as much as he could and felt better in spite of his dire situation.

That is until One-eye came back.

The gruff man had a sour expression on his face the likes of which Harvey had never seen. "You lied to me," One-eye said.

Harvey frowned. "What do you mean?" He grinned at the dark, tanned figure as best he could with his swollen cheek.

He knew exactly what One-eye meant. He had lied to protect Sariah, and he would do it again in a heartbeat. Sariah was worth anything, even whatever punishment lay in store for him next.

He'd been wondering exactly how long his little power play was going to buy him timewise. Not long, apparently.

One-eye stooped toward the ground and picked something up. In the darkened tent, Harvey couldn't make out what it was.

"You lied," One-eye repeated.

Harvey shook his head. "No, sir," he insisted. "I told the truth. I'm a miner from Chatwick, I swear it."

One-eye nodded. "Indeed, that part might be true. But you didn't come here with a group. The Chatwick miner group isn't due here for another two months. I know. I checked."

The hair on Harvey's neck stood on end. How could One-eye possibly know that? One-eye and his group were obviously quite well-connected. If they weren't, surely someone would have stopped them from yanking him in the daylight yesterday.

Harvey let out a tiny chuckle. "Mistaken identity?" he offered with a goofy grin. Inwardly, he was cowering in fear, but he wasn't about to let his captor see it.

One-eye, for his part, didn't seem to appreciate Harvey's sense of humor. He grinned back, but it was a grin full of malice and a promise of dark things to come.

"You lied," One-eye said one last time.

"You know, you say it often enough and maybe it will be true." It was a weak comeback, but it was all he had.

Meanwhile, One-eye was taking the object he'd picked up from the ground and wrapping it around his fist. Harvey could see it now the gruff bandit leader was closer. It looked like some sort of brass knuckle. A primitive version of one, perhaps, but effective all the same.

One-eye got really close and leaned in until his lips were practically touching Harvey's face and whispered,

"Now, you're going to see exactly what happens when someone lies to me."

Harvey did his best to look defiant. To his credit, he didn't even close his eyes when the first blow came and One-eye's brass-knuckled fist hit him square in the stomach.

The wind was knocked out of him from the force of the punch, which he supposed was a good thing because otherwise his scream would have lit up the night. He'd thought the pain from the slap earlier was bad, but this was so much worse.

Harvey crumpled. He was still tied to the pole so he couldn't fall over completely, but he managed to fall to his knees.

With every ounce of his body crying out in protest, Harvey made himself stand back up. Then he looked up at One-eye and grinned again as broadly as he could. "Is that all you got?"

The gruff bandit leader came at him again with another blow to his midsection. This one was even worse, and it knocked him almost to the ground.

He screamed, then, and the sound was terrible enough to wake the dead.

His entire body hurt with a pain unlike anything he'd ever experienced before, but he wasn't distraught, for his thoughts had turned to Sariah. At least she would remain safe. He could die knowing that.

Kneeling in the dim light of the tent, battered and beaten as he was and far away from everything he'd ever known, he could have sworn Sariah was right there with him, helping him through the pain and keeping him safe.

The thought made him smile.

Sariah took Gabriel's outstretched hand in her own.

"Hold tight," he said, pulling her in close.

It was well after dark. Sariah's training sessions had taken longer than she thought and it was almost midnight already. Gabe had been insistent they didn't have long if they were to have any chance of saving Harvey's life and had made them leave at once.

They used his magic once already to teleport outside of town and get past the gate guards without issue, and now he was teleporting them again.

Sariah had argued with him, of course, since Gabe told her earlier teleporting without knowing exactly where you were going was dangerous, but she was just giving him a hard time. Inwardly, she was grateful for him taking things so seriously.

Not that it had made any difference. Ever since Sariah had mentioned Harvey was holed up in a camp west of town, Gabe had gone into somewhat of a frenzy.

Harvey's kidnappers must mean business to have riled him up the way they had.

Gabe even left Bear behind, insisting it was too dangerous to bring the dog along where they were headed. Sariah had to admit, she was going to miss the mangy mutt. He'd really grown on her over the past few weeks, but Gabe wouldn't back down.

At least he'd had the forethought to bring all of their weapons with them, everything but the bow. He said if they ended up needing the bow in close quarters, they were in more trouble than a bow would fix for them.

Sariah marveled as the magic swirled around them once again and in the blink of an eye, they crossed great distances that would have taken hours on foot.

When she opened her eyes, she saw a massive tent city sprawled out in front of them. She swore there were as many tents in the city as there were in the whole of the market square, though that was probably an overstatement.

Regardless, whoever stayed there, they weren't simple-minded ruffians. They were going up against a veritable army with just the two of them. Not great odds.

Sariah gulped down her fear. What was she thinking, heading into an enemy camp with nothing but a couple of daggers and swords for defense? Was she mental? The enemy forces vastly outnumbered them, even with his magic.

"Relax," Gabe said from somewhere behind her. "If we do our job right, they'll never even know we were in there."

He smiled at her and she could just make it out in the dim light from the moon.

She frowned. "How so?"

Gabe's smile got bigger. "Mental magic, remember? We'll make them think we're not there. Most of them are probably asleep at this hour anyway."

Sariah nodded. She should have figured. It was a far more sensible approach than trying to take on the whole army.

She wasn't sure how she felt about using magic, even with Harvey's life on the line. Invisibility was the trick her parents' killer had used on her. She wasn't sure if using the same magic didn't make her as awful as her parent's killer. It was Gabe using the magic and not her, but somehow it didn't feel right.

Gabe was already walking along toward the camp, leaving her behind, so she didn't have any time to wallow in her own head. She really didn't want to be caught out here by herself.

The two walked as quietly and quickly as they could to the camp. Gabe had insisted they not talk unless absolutely necessary. He'd told her you could hide your words from other people like you could your physical appearance, but it took more effort to muffle sounds, and he was already using quite a bit of magic.

She wasn't about to argue. Being found out in the middle of the camp would definitely qualify as a worst-case scenario.

As they neared the bandit encampment, Sariah saw ornate banners flying over the entrance. The kidnappers weren't simple small-timers if they had banners announcing their presence, but it felt odd they'd announce it so brazenly.

She could barely make them out in the moonlight. The banners had a dust-colored raven with piercing blue eyes flying over a field in the nighttime. It was a weird sight since everyone knew ravens were black.

It was nothing she recognized, though Gabe seemed to. He nodded to her once and pointed to them as if the banners should mean something. She shrugged, and the two kept going.

Moments later, she could see two guards standing tall

at the gate of the tent complex. Their intense gaze filled the night, searching high and low for some sign of trouble. These guards weren't like the kind-hearted, gentle-natured sort she'd known back at home or even the monotone ones back in Stratton.

These guards meant business and wouldn't be easily fooled.

Her heart started beating faster and harder in her chest as they neared, but the two men didn't budge the closer they got. It appeared Gabe's magic was every bit as good as he'd promised it would be.

At one point, her heart was beating so hard she swore the two would be able to hear it, even if they couldn't see her, but the guards did nothing but search the ground and sky around them.

As she walked past, so close she could smell the stench of onions on the breath of the one on the right, she marveled these gate guards, undoubtedly confident in their abilities, really couldn't sense her.

Part of her wanted to do something silly, like wave her hands in front of their faces, but she was too scared to do anything but keep putting one foot in front of the other.

At last, they were past the guards, and likely the hardest part of their voyage. With front door guards like that, the bandits within probably had their guards down and slept soundly, figuring they'd have plenty of time to react to a disturbance.

Gabe pointed with two fingers toward a large-ish tent off to the side of the middle of the tent city. That was their destination, the fingers said. How he could possibly know was anyone's guess.

When they got out of this mess, if they got out of it, she corrected herself, Sariah was going to have to sit down and talk with Gabe more about his past. He knew too much about what was going on around here.

As quietly as they could, the two crept over to the tent, trying their best to steer clear of other tent openings and the occasional bandit who had fallen asleep in the middle of the thoroughfare.

The sight made Sariah's blood boil. Here these bandits were, sleeping off their fun and liquor on the ground without a care in the world after they'd beaten her Harvey. It simply wasn't fair.

She desperately wanted to do something about it and to settle the score. She pulled on Gabe's shirtsleeve and he looked back at her expectantly, a little annoyed.

Sariah pointed to a bandit sprawled out in front of her and made a sawing motion across her neck.

Gabe's eyes grew wide in shock and he shook his head no.

Sariah scowled at him and made furious motions with her hands. She even pouted, but Gabe was insistent in his denial.

As much as she wanted to pay these bandits back pound for pound for the pain they'd caused Harvey, she understood his viewpoint. If someone came across the dead body of a bandit while they were still busy rescuing Harvey, the camp would be alerted to their presence.

Then they'd need rescuing, too, or worse. She supposed their comeuppance would have to happen later, but she swore then and there their time would come. Someday in the future, whoever these guys worked for would pay for hurting her friend.

The rest of the way to the tent passed without incident. The tent wasn't guarded, so they were able to slip inside easily.

Inside was even darker than outside, but Sariah made out a crumpled form kneeling on the ground and tied to a pole. His face was practically touching the dirt and his arms were tied up behind him, keeping him from falling over completely.

"Harvey!" Sariah cried, breaking the silence rule. She didn't care. Her friend was in pain, and she'd finally found him.

Gabe opened his mouth to object but said nothing. Probably too proud to break the no silence rule, even to yell at her, she supposed. Just as well.

She raced over to Harvey's side and picked up his head with her hands. Even in the dim light, she could tell his face was bruised and bloody. The rest of him didn't look much better. But he was breathing and still warm, so at least he was alive.

Harvey coughed a couple of times and fresh blood spilled out of his mouth. With weak eyes, he looked up at his savior. "Sariah?" he said, sounding confused. "What are you doing out here? Did they catch you too?"

Sariah chuckled and shook her head. "No, silly, I've come to rescue you," she replied in a hushed tone. She'd made the mistake of being loud once already. No need to call extra attention to themselves.

Harvey coughed again and looked at her with equal parts reverence and excitement. "Rescue me? Why would I want a rescue from a swanky joint like this?" He gave her one of his signature dopey grins.

Sariah frowned at him. "Now, now. This is no time to be glib. We have to get you out of here."

Harvey pointed with his chin as best he could at the leather bonds tying him to the pole. "I thought you liked me all tied up," he offered wryly.

"Stop it, you. You're being rescued and that's that. We can talk about other things later."

"Ooh, promise?"

Sariah shook her head, then took out one of her daggers. Not the assassin's blade. She'd not sully Harvey's rescue with a blade that held such malice. With the dagger, she started sawing at Harvey's bonds.

Harvey coughed another couple of times and kept staring at her. "Aw, come on. What are people going to think if you rescue me? I'm not some damsel in distress you know."

Sariah smiled at him. "I have a dress. You can wear it for me next time if it makes you feel better."

"Stop playing around, you two! We need to get a move on," Gabe hissed. He was standing nearer the tent entrance and looking around.

Harvey pointed his eyes in Gabe's direction. "What's got his panties all in a bunch?"

Sariah shrugged. "Him? He's always like that. Such a downer."

"Come on!" Gabe insisted.

Sariah and Harvey giggled.

She cut the last of the bonds and then she was through. Her friend was free.

Harvey rubbed his wrists where the bonds had dug into them and tried to stand. He was semi-successful with Sariah's help.

She put her arm around Harvey's midsection to help steady him and ended up touching the wound in his side, which made him wince and growl in pain. She needed help. She wasn't going to get him very far like this.

Sariah motioned for Gabe to come over and help him instead. Gabe and Harvey were of a similar height.

Gabe took in the entirety of Harvey's battered form the best he could in the low light. "Are you going to be all right walking out of here?" he asked.

Harvey pounded his chest weakly with one hand. "Who me? Never better."

"Oh, stop it. Let's get you out of here."

But their trip to freedom was cut drastically short, for at the same moment a tall, gruff man with one eye came into the tent with another man close at his heels.

"The brat is in here," One-eye was saying to the other man as he entered.

Everyone blinked a couple times. It was hard to say which side was more surprised to see the other.

Sariah screamed something unintelligible and did the only thing she could think of, she took the knife in her hand and flung it at one of the two men.

The dagger's flight path rang true and ended up sticking into One-eye's face next to his good eye. The gruff man howled in pain and put a hand over his fresh wound as he drew his blade with the other. The other man was almost too startled to do anything but managed to draw his blade as well.

What happened next was so fast Sariah barely caught it all in the dark, dim light of the tent.

Gabriel sprang into action. His blade was in his hand faster than should have been humanly possible. With a few quick swipes of his sword, Gabe impaled the one startled bandit and disarmed One-eye.

He made rubbing motions with his free hand, and a fireball formed in his open palm, which he thrust at One-eye. The man's clothing erupted in flames as the gruff bandit leader backed out of the tent and spilled out into the thoroughfare.

His clothes were still burning as One-eye ran about and then flung himself into the dirt, catching the corner of Harvey's tent on fire at the same time.

Sariah, Harvey, and Gabe could hear the sounds of motion across the bandit encampment. Everyone seemed to either see or hear the bandit leader flailing about, and several of them started rushing their way to either put out the flames or see what had caused the disturbance.

Sariah looked around with fear in her eyes. They had managed to get in here and get Harvey easily enough, but the way out was well and truly blocked. There'd be no going back the same way.

She looked up at Gabriel. "Can you get us out of here?" she asked.

The older man looked back at her with tired eyes. He was completely spent from all the magic and the short melee. "I can try," he offered. "No guarantee it will work, but I guess it's better than nothing."

Sariah nodded. "That's all I can ask."

"Stand super tight, everyone."

Harvey hobbled over as best he could.

Maybe it was better like this. It was obvious Harvey wouldn't get far on his feet as injured as he was.

Sariah hugged Gabriel tight around the middle with one arm and grasped Harvey's arm with the other. Together, they must have made quite the sight.

"Here goes nothing." All three of them squeezed their eyes shut while Gabe called upon his magic one last time, giving it all he had.

When they opened their eyes again, they were back in the spot they'd been at when they'd first emerged from the teleport and seen the bandit camp off in the distance. It was still there, though it was far more active than it had been before.

Flames from somewhere near the middle of the encampment arced high through the still night air, engulfing one of the main tents in its destructive force. All around the camp, Sariah could hear the sounds of men shouting.

She watched the carnage play out in the moonlight as her two companions slumped to the ground, exhausted but safe at last.

As the flames climbed higher, the corners of her mouth curled into a smile and one thought reverberated in her head. Payback's a bitch, ain't it?

CHAPTER FIFTEEN

It had been about two weeks since the incident at the bandit camp and Sariah still hadn't gotten answers to any of her questions out of Gabriel. She'd tried, but he'd remained firmly tight-lipped.

Sariah was determined. It was going to change tonight, and she was going to get him talking one way or another.

The past two weeks had been interesting. That first night they'd all slept out in the fields with the fires of the bandit camp in the background. It was risky, but Harvey could barely move, and Gabe had been too exhausted from the extended magic use to do much of anything.

Fortunately, nothing happened. The bandits were too busy with their own problems to be moving around causing new ones.

The next day they made a makeshift stretcher out of a shirt and a couple of downed branches and started the grueling task of carrying Harvey back into town.

Gabe had offered to teleport them, but Sariah had refused. She still wasn't keen on magic use if it wasn't absolutely necessary, and the two of them could march just fine on their own.

They didn't get very far, and eventually Sariah gave in and let Gabe teleport them. He got them to the edge of the town with his magic but no further. He had said it would be too dangerous to teleport them into the middle of the town with people walking about.

Then Gabe had healed Harvey the little he could with his waning strength so he could walk through the front gate. Sariah had been worried, but they made it through without any issues.

The same guard from before, Ty was there again when they came through. Gabe whispered a few words in his ear and they'd been waved through without issue. Sariah was really starting to wonder about that relationship. She'd have to press Gabe further about it when she had a chance, but it could wait.

Once they were safe, sound, and well-rested, Gabe had gotten to the task of healing Harvey properly. He worked his magic carefully and stopped once Harvey was able to walk without much pain.

Her best friend had been too proud to let Gabe heal him the rest of the way, even though she'd told him it was okay.

Sariah wondered if it was out of deference to her feelings on magic. Most likely he was just stubborn and showy. She certainly wouldn't put it past him.

From then until now they'd stuck to town, waiting for Harvey to heal fully and not doing much else.

Gabe had offered to continue her magic training with new skills in their downtime, but she'd refused. Even if the stuff had gotten them out of a very sticky situation and helped save Harvey, she couldn't trust its powers fully.

There was one trick she practiced with him time and again, connecting minds and sensing the other person's location. That little trick had proved invaluable and would come in handy if their trio ever got separated again.

She was getting good at the spell, to the point where she could even connect with random strangers on the street. Not that she liked doing it. Strangers' minds could be...icky.

The time had passed slowly. There'd been no sight of additional bandits in town since the incident, and no news about her parents' killer, either. It had been boring waiting for Harvey to feel better.

Now that he was running around on his own again, the three of them could get moving. But not before Gabe talked.

Right now, she was on her way to Gabe's room in The Dragonfly. He'd insisted on getting a separate room for himself after the incident to let Harvey heal in peace. More likely he just didn't like Sariah's constant badgering.

She had been patient enough, and patience wasn't her strong suit to begin with. The silence ended tonight.

With her head held high and her back straight in a confident position, she knocked on Gabe's door. It took a moment, but she soon heard the sounds of shuffling feet and a grumbly voice that signaled life on the other side of the wooden barrier.

"Who is it?" Gabe's voice called.

"I think you know damn well who it is. Does anyone

else even knock on your stupid door? You're not exactly popular."

Maybe not the best way to start the night's conversation, she thought.

Still, it seemed to do the trick. The door handle turned a moment later and Gabe's head peeped out of a crack between the door and the wall. "Yes, Sariah? What is it at this hour?"

She batted her eyes at him. "Oh, I'm sorry, were you sleeping?" she asked in the sweetest tone she could muster.

In fairness, it was almost midnight. Of course he'd been sleeping.

She didn't give him time to respond. Instead, she reached forward with one hand, grabbed hold of his tunic, and pulled as hard as she could until his face was practically level with her own.

"Well too bad, sweet cheeks," she spat at him. "You're talking. You know more than you let on about the bandits who took Harvey. Time to spill." No one could fault her for not being direct.

Gabe grabbed her hand and squeezed gently until she let go. With his other hand, he rubbed his eyes and pulled on his face. "You're not going to let me go back to sleep, are you?" he replied.

Sariah shook her head and smiled at him.

He rolled his eyes. "Very well. I guess I do owe you an explanation." He opened his door further and made a motion for her to come forward. "Come on in and have a seat. This might take a bit."

She nodded once and entered.

Once they were both in the room, Gabe shut the door.

He motioned for Sariah to sit on the bed, which she did, then he paced back and forth and looked around shiftily.

"Where to start, where to start," he said a few times.

Sariah placed her hands on the bed and sat up straighter. "You could always start at the beginning, you know."

He grinned at her. "Okay, fair enough. One day, my mom and dad were feeling rather frisky, and…"

"Oh, stop it, you perv!" Sariah shouted at him and threw a pillow at his head for good measure, which he unfortunately dodged.

Gabe held up his hand in front of him to get her to stop. "Okay, okay. You're right, that was stupid of me." He took a few more steps then finally stopped and sat on the other bed. "I said you deserve the truth and you do."

He cracked his neck muscles and inhaled deeply. "Have you ever heard of an organization known as the Dusk Ravens?"

Sariah wrinkled her nose. "No, I don't think so. Should I have?"

Gabe chuckled. "I suppose not. No reason you'd get involved with them in that little town of yours."

"Hey!" She grabbed another pillow and held it menacingly.

He held up his hand again. "Sorry. Please don't throw another pillow."

She whined but put it back.

"Thank you. Anyway, on paper the Dusk Ravens are a merchant organization. A trader's guild, if you would. They control the trade routes in this region and broker all the big trade deals. A majority of the merchants you see in a town like this one are allied with the Dusk Ravens. Frankly, it'd be stupid not to, as it would make it hard to find a trade partner."

Sariah nodded. "That makes sense, I guess. But what does a trade organization have to do with any of this?"

"I was getting to that." Gabe cleared his throat. "You see, their public presence might be benevolent, but underneath, the Dusk Ravens are rotten to the core. They secure their power through some highly unseemly methods."

"Like banditry?"

Gabe nodded. "Exactly like banditry. That banner we saw at the camp? It's one of theirs. They control the bandit groups that roam around both inside and outside town, and anyone found trading goods who isn't a member of the Dusk Ravens' organization is fair game on the open roads."

Sariah's eyes grew wide in disgust. "That's despicable."

"Perhaps, but it's also quite effective."

"Doesn't anyone ever try and stop them?"

Gabe chuckled. "How do you stop the most powerful force in town? Don't get me wrong, it's not like people don't try, but no one has their manpower. The Dusk Ravens have a veritable army of thugs. No one merchant stands a chance against odds like that."

Sariah slumped. "I guess when you put it that way, it makes sense."

Gabe cleared his throat. "That's not all. Remember earlier how I said most magic teachers are bad people? I wasn't kidding. Magic instruction is a highly guarded secret, and the Dusk Ravens control that, too. You can't learn magic in these parts unless you sign a contract with them. It's another way they hold onto their power."

Sariah cocked her head to the side. "But you're a magic user and you're not one of them," she pointed out.

"Heh. Yeah. About that. That's the other part I was going to mention."

Sariah suddenly felt very uncomfortable. She shrunk back on the bed as far as she could until her back hit the wall. "You don't mean to say you…"

"Was!" Gabe shouted. "I was allied with them once, a long time ago. I've changed since."

She let herself relax. "What happened, then? What changed you?"

Gabe sighed. "My old mentor, if you can believe it. When I met Jakob, everything changed. He was so different from the people I knew in the Dusk Ravens organization. He showed me a different path. A better one."

"So that was that? You just up and quit?"

Gabe shook his head. "Not exactly. You don't just quit the Dusk Ravens. No doubt they've been trying to hunt me down. Once upon a time I'd dreamed of taking them down, but that's not likely to ever happen. So I hid out instead."

Sariah's eyes rolled back into her head. "Oh, so that's why you're always looking over your shoulder, and keep your magic a secret."

He nodded. "Yep."

"I guess it makes sense now."

"There is one more thing I've meant to talk to you about."

Sariah's head was buzzing with all the new information as it was. She couldn't believe there was yet another revelation. "Go on," she said hesitantly.

Gabe sighed once, then twice. "Actually, I'm not sure

now is the best time. Maybe tomorrow, when we're all more awake, I…"

She shot up off the bed and got in his face. "Oh no you don't! You're coming clean right now. I had to wait two whole weeks for this much. Spit it out!"

He backed up and held his hands out to protect himself. "Okay, okay. It's just, you might want to sit back down for this."

"What could possibly be so shocking after all of that information I'd need to sit down?"

"It's about your parents' killer."

That stopped her cold. Her blood drained from her face and she almost fell backward onto the floor but stopped herself just in time. "What about him?" she managed through clenched teeth.

He took in a deep breath. "He was a Dusk Raven. At least, I think he was."

Sariah was very upset. The same organization responsible for Harvey's torment had been responsible for her parents' deaths, too? She had to know.

"How would you -"

"Know for sure?" Gabe finished. "The only way to know for sure would be to check his right hand for a small raven tattoo." He held out his hand. "Here, like this one."

Sariah inspected his palm. Sure enough, there was a raven tattoo on it. It was small and almost impossible to see in the dim light, but it was there.

"That doesn't exactly do me a lot of good."

"No, I guess not," Gabe admitted. "But there are other ways to check. The dagger you carry around with you, the assassin's blade? If he was a Dusk Raven, it should have a raven emblem on the hilt. Go on, check."

Sariah instantly dug her hands beneath her clothes and reached for the blade she kept strapped to her leg. She never took it off, even at bedtime. It was the only thing she had to identify the killer with, so it was far too precious to let go.

Her hands wrapped around it and she practically tore it loose. She scanned the length of the hilt in the dim light of the room.

Her eyes grew wide and a pit formed in the bottom of her stomach. On the pommel of the blade, carved in exquisite detail, was the image of a raven in mid-flight.

Lucien hurried through the halls of the complex on the heels of the attendant Daniel. He was excited to be here for once, and was annoyed with the servant's slower pace. Part of him wanted to kick Daniel to speed the man up, but he knew that would earn him no favors, and he had no desire to upset the Master.

His last encounter had gone swimmingly. He'd returned the missing gemstones from the ancient amulet and reported on the bitch's almost-certain doom. The Master had been quite pleased with how things had turned out.

Now Lucien was back, having been summoned once more. This could only mean good things were in store for him. He was sure of it.

He wondered what mission the Master would put him on next. Whatever it was, he was convinced it would be thrilling and important. He was one of the favorite assassins, after all. Not just any assignment would come his way. It would have to be quite the assignment to be worthy of his esteem.

That was what he told himself as he made his way through the maze of tunnels behind Daniel.

A moment later, Daniel stopped in front of a nondescript door and ushered Lucien on in. With a slight scoff at the helper, he complied.

Once inside, he was shocked by what he saw. The Master was before him, this time looking like a wizened old man with stark white hair, pale, sallow skin, and a hooked nose. That wasn't surprising. The Master always changed his appearance.

What was surprising was they weren't alone. Someone else was in the room with the two of them, someone he didn't recognize.

Could the Master be sending me on a joint mission? he wondered. It didn't make any sense. He was an assassin, trained to move in the shadows and alone in the darkness. Why would he be given a companion?

The Master beckoned with one pockmarked hand for Lucien to kneel before him. He bit down on his tongue to hold back the fear forming in his spine and complied. Good or bad, it wouldn't do to keep the Master waiting.

"Welcome back, Lucien," the Master called out. His voice was surprisingly soft and melodical, not at all matching his outward appearance. The dissonance was unnerving, probably on purpose.

"Wh-what task do you have for me today, Master?" Lucien asked with a slight stutter. He chided himself for showing even a hint of his fear. He should know better by now.

The Master didn't seem to notice, or at least didn't care and kept going. "Lucien, please recount the details of your mission once more and leave nothing out."

He looked up then with surprise in his eyes. "Master?"

"For the newcomer to hear." The old man clarified with a grand wave of his hand.

Lucien nodded. He didn't believe the Master would have forgotten a single detail but relating the tale to someone new made sense.

He took in a deep breath and told of his two separate missions into Chatwick, starting with locating the girl outside the mineshaft and ending with him setting the bitch's little house on fire.

The Master seemed to take especially careful notice of the girl's appearance and had Lucien repeat back several details such as eye and skin color several times. It was an odd request, but he saw no reason not to oblige.

"You're positive the girl died in the house fire?" the Master asked as Lucien finished.

The young assassin nodded and grinned from ear to ear. "Yes, Master. There was no way she could have escaped the blaze. I took great care to block all the exits."

The Master looked down on him with a look that did not show an ounce of pity. He placed a cracked, wrinkled hand on Lucien's shoulder and grabbed it tightly. The old man's grip was surprisingly strong, and the yellowing nails dug into Lucien's skin even through his shirt.

Lucien winced in pain but otherwise kept his composure. He was determined to leave a good impression.

"Poor, misguided assassin," the Master said then. As he spoke, he dug his nails into Lucien's shoulder even further until blood started to pour from the tiny wounds they made.

"I'm sorry, Master. I...I don't understand," Lucien responded, trying hard to fight through the pain to the point tears were forming in his eyes.

"You told me the girl was dead, did you not?"

He nodded once more, though he was more confused and uncertain as the moments passed by.

"How I wish that were the case." The Master eased his grip on Lucien's shoulder then and waved at the other member of the room, who had remained completely motionless with head bowed up until then. "Severin, please relate what you told me yesterday."

The man known as Severin raised his head to reveal the freak show that was his face. To start, the newcomer only had one eye. A massive, old scar on his face covered where the other eye used to be. There was a fresh scar on his other cheek that couldn't have been more than two weeks old.

Worse, part of his face appeared to have practically melted off his skull, like he'd been caught in a fire and hadn't been able to escape in time. The sight was gruesome.

In spite of his resolve, Lucien shuddered at the sight. He wondered why the man hadn't sought out a healer. Surely, the Master would have helped someone he held in enough regard to hold audience with. Perhaps this Severin preferred things this way. That was an even darker thought.

Severin began speaking in a tone both gruff and raw, like someone being raked over gravel. The man spoke of a routine kidnapping and ransom operation gone horribly wrong, and of a seemingly helpless young man with powerful magician friends who set him free and destroyed an entire bandit camp in the process.

All of which was shocking, to be sure, but Lucien only half-listened to the sordid tale as he wondered what it had to do with him. That was until Severin mentioned the girl.

There had been a girl among the saviors. A small thing with short brown hair and hazel eyes, whose description matched the girl he'd been sent twice now to kill.

Lucien backed away as the revelation dawned on him. He'd failed the Master. Not just once, but twice now. His eyes darted toward the exit of the room and then back, but even that half-second was too long.

The Master shot out one of his hands and grasped Lucien's head in a clawed embrace. Once again, his nails bit into Lucien's skin as the old man forcibly lifted his head until Lucien's eyes met his own.

"Tell me, Lucien," the Master spoke. "What good is an assassin who cannot manage to kill his target?"

Lucien had to strive to work his jaw, the grip on it was so tight. Slowly, the words started to come. "I-I'm sorry, Master! Please, forgive me!" he implored. "I-I'll make it right this time, I swear it!"

The Master shoved Lucien's head away with enough force it sent the young assassin sprawling onto the ground.

"Why should I let you? You've failed me twice. Surely, I've been more than reasonable."

Lucien scrambled to his feet and looked again at the

Master. Where there had once been gentleness and pity, he saw only rage. "Please, Master! I'll succeed this time, I swear it! I will, or I'll-"

He tried to think of something he could offer, anything he could do to temper the man's anger and give Lucien a chance to breathe another breath as a free man. Only one thought came to him.

"I'll volunteer for your experiments!" he offered at last.

That gave the Master pause. He rubbed his chin thoughtfully for a moment. "A volunteer, you say? I could do a lot with a willing participant."

Lucien nodded. "Yes, Master. I will volunteer." As he spoke the words, he knew he'd sealed his own doom. If even half the rumors he'd heard were true, being signed up for the Master's twisted experiments was a fate far worse than death.

"Very well," the Master said at last. "Now leave, and don't come back without solid proof the task is complete. Or, well, I think we all know what will happen."

The Master gave him a broad, sickening grin and shooed him away with a hand.

Lucien nodded once more and left the room. Several minutes later, when he was finally out of the complex, his breathing and heart rate slowed to a normal pace. He had made a grim deal with the Master, and it was one he had every intention of fulfilling.

CHAPTER SIXTEEN

"You have to help me stop them!" Sariah insisted.

Gabriel groaned. It was only about the twentieth time she'd said that in the past day. Ever since he'd opened up about his sordid past with the Dusk Ravens, she'd been insufferable, insisting the three of them do what they could to bring the organization down.

He supposed he could understand her viewpoint, to a degree. The Dusk Ravens had been responsible for her parents' deaths, the loss of her house, and even kidnapped her best friend. To a sixteen year old, that was practically losing your entire life.

If he were to put himself in her shoes, he'd probably want the same thing. He did, and it wasn't even his life that had gotten ruined. But he knew better. There was no taking down an organization with that kind of power. Avoiding it was the only reasonable answer.

"No," Gabe replied in a weary tone.

"Aww," Sariah whined. "But you have to help me!"

He sighed and pulled on his face to bring life back into

his cheeks. He was tired, having barely slept the night before. Sariah hadn't been interested in letting him get any shuteye after his revelation and had kept him up half the night discussing overly detailed plans to bring about the Dusk Ravens' downfall.

It was cute, in a way. She was really fired up. Not that any of her ideas, like going to the authorities with proof of Harvey's kidnapping, would work. The Dusk Ravens had every local ruler in their back pocket. No amount of cajoling or arguing would get them anywhere.

He'd told her as much, several times. Even Harvey had tried to talk her down, much to the kid's credit. He'd had no more success. Sariah was quite stubborn when she wanted to be.

"Not really," Gabe fired back. The argument was starting to sound wooden and forced, but what else could he do? He was in no hurry to throw his life away, let alone hers.

"But you promised!" she demanded. "You said you'd help me take down my parents' killer back in Chatwick. You promised!"

Gabe rolled his eyes. "Not this again. Yes, I promised to help you take down the assassin, but that was it. My assistance stops there. If you want to go running about throwing your life away after, that's on you."

"Humph!" Sariah turned on her heels and walked to the other side of the small room to where Harvey was sitting. Gabe watched the kid put a hand on Sariah's shoulder and whisper something in her ear. Undoubtedly the kid was trying to soothe her nerves or calm her down. Gabe could only hope the other man was successful.

The two sat talking in hushed tones and giving each other furtive glances, then Sariah came back over to him.

"Fine," she said in a tone that made it perfectly clear she didn't believe anything of the sort. "We'll finish our hunt for the assassin, then go our separate ways." The girl had her hand stuck out in front of her in an offering of peace.

Gabe took the offered hand and gave it a hearty shake. "Fine," he repeated.

That wasn't at all what he wanted. He still wanted to train her. There was so much he could do with someone of her potential. Maybe even topple the Dusk Ravens someday. If only she'd listen and stop doing such brash things, but when she was in this mood, he knew he'd never convince her to take things slow.

Maybe all wasn't lost. Her emotions were running hot right now, but once things settled down, she'd see the light of day. There was still hope, he just needed to wait her out.

"So," Gabe said. "Where does that leave us?"

"We still need to find out where Sariah's killer lives." Harvey chimed in.

Sariah nodded. "Yes. Any ideas?"

Gabe rubbed his chin. "Well, we're pretty sure he's a Dusk Raven, right?"

The other two nodded.

"That's more information than we had before. Maybe he belonged to the bandit encampment? Perhaps we already took him down and didn't even realize it." He didn't believe it himself, but it was worth a shot. He really just wanted to get back to training her. She'd be far better off in a battle with a magician if she'd train more.

Sariah scoffed. "No." Her tone had a finality that said it wasn't worth arguing the point.

He pushed anyway. "How do we know for sure? It's not like we explored the whole camp."

She shook her head violently. "He wasn't there. I would have known. I would have felt him there."

Gabe side-eyed her. "Are you sure about that?"

She folded her arms, gave him an icy glare, and said nothing.

Who knows, maybe she would have felt him, Gabe thought. It was possible. She'd manifested magical talent without trying before, so it could happen again.

It didn't really matter, though. She was most likely right. A trained killer like that wouldn't associate with the ruffians who inhabited that kind of camp. He would consider those types to be well below him in rank and stature. There was no chance the killer had been there.

"Fair enough," Gabe relented. "It's still more information than we had to go on before."

Harvey offered a suggestion. "Maybe someone in town would know where to find the local Dusk Ravens?"

Gabe laughed hard. "A local? Rat on a Dusk Raven? No one in town is that level of crazy. Sorry, kid, but no."

"Hey!" Sariah said. "At least he's doing more than sitting on his ass!"

Gabe winced. It was a low blow, considering the only reason he was sitting down was that Sariah had kept him up half the night, but she wasn't wrong. "No one in town is going to turn on the Dusk Ravens. It's like I told you yesterday. They control the trade routes and the government. Who's going to go against that much power?" He made a dismissive motion with his hand. "Besides, you'd have to find someone who's both well connected and not a Dusk Raven first. Good luck with that."

Gabe looked at Sariah. She had a thoughtful look on her face like she had an idea and knew just what to do next. It was a look that always ended with someone in trouble. He shuddered to think what it could be this time.

"Someone who's well connected but not a Dusk Raven, eh?" she repeated.

He turned to face the wall. "Yep. Like such a person would even exist."

"Actually, I think they just might. Thanks, Gabe!"

Gabe opened his mouth to say something witty when he heard the door to the room creak open. A knot of fear gathered in his gut and he turned back around fast, but Sariah was already gone.

"Wait!" he cried, but it was too late.

Gabe shot an evil look at Harvey. "Why didn't you stop her?" he demanded.

Harvey gave him a goofy grin and just shrugged. "Like I could?"

The kid had a point. There was no stopping Sariah no matter what either one of them did.

"Besides," Harvey offered. " Bear went with her."

Just then, Gabe noticed the animal was no longer resting near his feet. "Bear!" he called after his dog. "You come back here this instant or no more bacon for you!" The dog was long gone, too.

Sariah and Bear practically ran through the city streets. It was starting to get late and, while they weren't worried about bandit attacks for the time being, there was a very real possibility the merchants would go home at a decent hour.

After they'd gone about half the distance to the market square, Sariah finally looked over her shoulder to see if anyone was following her. Much to her surprise, no one was.

Had she gotten away with her little gambit? Maybe.

Still, Gabe was a magician, and if she could use magic to find someone, then he could, too. He could track her down and drag her back if he really wanted to.

All the more reason to hurry, then, she thought with a smile.

She knew where she was going. It was the only place that made sense. She knew now both why the old dress-maker's stall had been so empty and why the shop owner had taken on such an odd expression when she'd seen the assassin's dagger.

Valerie wasn't one of them. She wasn't allied with the Dusk Ravens, but she knew about them. Maybe, just maybe, she'd know enough. It was a slim hope, but it was all Sariah had to go on, and that was better than nothing.

As she and Bear passed the fountain by the entrance and the market square came into view, the two slowed down. She was far enough ahead of any pursuers now they wouldn't catch up before she could disappear in the throngs of people, and she was almost out of breath anyway.

Sariah watched the crowds of people come and go in

the market square and for a moment she doubted her purpose here.

What if Gabe was right and the Dusk Ravens really were that powerful? She wondered if it a good idea to bring someone innocent into the mix.

Suddenly, she wasn't very sure. Valerie had been so nice to her when she'd come into town. She had given her clothing and a shoulder to cry on and had asked for nothing in return. If the Dusk Ravens were as awful as Gabriel made them out to be, she didn't deserve to be bogged down in this enterprise.

There could end up being retribution. The Dusk Ravens had a lot of bad people under their employ, and one little merchant in a big town wouldn't exactly be missed.

She shook her head and hardened her resolve. Even if all the bad rumors were true, Sariah didn't believe anyone would ever connect the two of them together. No, Valerie would be safe. There was also the chance the old woman wouldn't answer any questions to begin with.

Sariah wondered if this could be a trap, a ruse to get her to drop her guard, but that didn't make sense. She couldn't believe someone as sweet as Valerie could be evil. Sariah was just letting her own doubts delay the inevitable.

Here she was, moments from potentially finding her parents' killer and ending her quest that she'd started on all those weeks ago, and now she had cold feet. She didn't know what she was afraid of, except maybe Gabe would make good on his promise and leave her alone afterward.

Pfft, good on him if he does. I don't need him anyway, she thought.

Deep down, she knew better. She wasn't ready for this

chapter of her life to close. He had power, and access to money and resources she didn't have. It wasn't like she had a lot to hold onto at this point in her life.

She wasn't sure that was it, and she only wanted him around for his resources. She thought there may be more to it. She shook her head. Such thoughts would do her no good now. She had to keep moving forward.

Sariah dipped into the throng of people and let the wave propel her forward past several stalls. Though they were filled with fine foods and exquisite, hand-crafted goods, she paid them no heed. She knew exactly where she was headed and why. Such trivial things were of no consequence.

A few minutes later, she and Bear emerged from the throng onto the far side of the market square. In front of her lay the row of stalls she'd seen her first day here, the foodstuffs merchant off to the left and to the right her target, the dress merchant Valerie.

Another dress made of that same shimmery material she'd fallen in love with before, she thought it might be silk, lay at the entrance to the stall. It was blue instead of red, and every bit as gorgeous.

She let herself get distracted by the dress, to stall her task for just a moment longer and admire the handiwork. Would she ever find an excuse to wear her dress, she wondered. She couldn't imagine many instances where it would happen. Marriage, maybe.

"May I help you, miss?" An elderly voice called from within the tent.

Sariah smiled. It was Valerie's voice. The dress merchant was here. She wasn't too late.

"I've just come to admire the fabrics," Sariah replied. She heard the sounds of rummaging and movement from within the tent.

"Very well, then, make yourself at home. Let me know if you find any-" the words stopped short as Valerie locked eyes with Sariah.

"You," Valerie said slowly. The elderly woman backed away as she spoke the words.

It looked to Sariah like the elderly woman was scared, though she couldn't fathom why. She stepped forward and smiled as broadly as she could to try and put her at ease. "Oh good, you're here. I wanted to thank you properly for your kindness earlier."

Her efforts were for naught. Valerie backed up a step further, bumping into a table and spilling some of the fabrics into the dust on the ground. The woman grabbed hold of something hard on the table. "You shouldn't have," she said through clenched teeth. "Really, your thanks is all I need." She gave Sariah a weak smile.

Sariah took another step forward and Valerie showed what was in her hands. It was a small knife used for cutting fabric. She brandished it before her. "Come now, I paid my debt to your kind last time. Please, take whatever you want and leave me alone!"

Valerie was visibly shaking as she spoke. It was obvious the older woman was scared out of her wits.

Then it snapped into place. The dagger from earlier. Valerie must have thought Sariah was a Dusk Raven. Sariah shook her head and took another big step forward. "No, you misunderstand! I'm not one of them, I'm hunting them!"

Valerie blinked a few times. "I'm sorry, dearie, what?"

Sariah nodded. "It's true. I'm after the Dusk Ravens. I intend to make them pay for what they did to me."

The older woman laughed. "That's a good one, but you'll not fool me so easily."

Sariah frowned. "No, it's true. I'm not one of them, I'm after them."

Valerie just shook her head. "Look dearie, I like you, but if you don't leave my stall this instant, I might have to do something drastic." She brandished the knife in her hand again, which was still shaking violently.

"No, it's true. I promise!" Sariah insisted. She stuck out her palm. "Look! No tattoo. I'm telling the truth."

Valerie's eyes narrowed and she squinted to examine Sariah's palm. When she seemed satisfied there were no ravens, she visibly relaxed and let the knife drop. "Maybe you are telling the truth after all," she said.

Nodding, Sariah continued. "I am. And I do intend to stop them, but I need your help."

The older woman shook her head. "Oh you sweet thing. How innocent you must be. No one takes on the Dusk Ravens and lives to tell the tale. Even if I could help, why would I, dearie? I've built a decent life. I've no desire to throw it away."

They must be as bad as Gabe made them out to be, Sariah thought. Even this lone shopkeeper was scared stiff.

Sariah shook her head again. "It's not like that. All I need is information. I'll handle the rest."

"And even supposing I had this information you need so desperately, why would I give it to you?" Valerie countered.

"What do you mean?" Sariah cocked her head to the side.

The older woman placed a hand gingerly on Sariah's shoulder. "As I said earlier, I like you. Why would I help you throw your life away? Especially when it could end up costing my own in the process. No, there's no profit in that approach." She turned and walked away.

Sariah didn't back down. "Is that all life is to you? Profit?"

Valerie turned and gave her a weak smile. "It keeps many a mouth fed, dearie."

Sariah scoffed. "That's a bleary outlook on life!"

The older woman nodded. "Aye, but it's one sees me safe in my bed every evening."

"Come on," Sariah pressed. "You helped me earlier. What I told you earlier, about what the assassin did to my parents, and my home. All of that really happened. I have nothing left. Nothing but a slim hope of striking back and making a difference." She could see her words were starting to have an impact.

Valerie bowed her head. "Please. I'm a humble merchant, and I'm content. Please, leave me be, and pretend we never met. Take another dress if it will help ease your sadness. Just let this drop. You don't know what you're getting yourself into. Trust me on this."

Sariah tried to stand firm, but her resolve faltered and her legs gave way. If it wasn't for Bear standing next to her, she might have fallen over. "Please," she begged, a tear forming. "It's all I have left."

The older woman let out a deep sigh. She raised her

head and looked deep into Sariah's eyes and saw all of the sadness that lay there. She gave her a look of great pity.

Valerie darted her eyes about in all directions and motioned for Sariah to lean in close. "I shouldn't be tellin' ya this, dearie, but you leave me little choice. I overheard a few of them talking the other day when they were buying goods next door. They spoke about a complex not three days' march east of here," she said slowly in a hushed tone.

"It's hidden underneath a 'ruin of the old world,' they claimed. Said a couple of their big wigs and someone they called the Master made a base there a few years back." She dropped her voice even lower until it was hard to hear her speak. "If your assassin is one of them, he could be holed up there I suppose."

Sariah's eyes brightened. "Really?" she said aloud.

Valerie nodded. "Yes, dearie. Now don't ask me for nothing further. I've put us both at risk more than you know with just that little tidbit, and I don't even know for myself if it's true."

"Thank you!" Sariah beamed. She threw her arms around the older woman in a big embrace, then pulled away.

"What was that for, dearie?"

"For helping me out, of course."

Valerie chuckled. "Yes, well I'm still not sure I should have done that. Now be gone, and don't ever come back here, you understand? There are eyes and ears everywhere."

Sariah nodded. "Understood."

Valerie watched as the young girl known as Sariah bounded off back out of the tent, her dog in tow. Had she done the right thing, she wondered? There was really no way for her to know for sure.

She shrugged. It didn't matter. It's not like she'd ever see the girl again, anyway, right?

People like her were a dime a dozen, headstrong and brazen, never stopping to think about how their actions would affect others. Those people never stood a chance against the odds stacked against them. They never came home.

Still, maybe this Sariah person had a chance. She seemed different. More determined, and also more motivated. Maybe, just maybe, this time would also be different.

An old woman could dream.

CHAPTER SEVENTEEN

Lucien headed toward the town of Stratton. It would be a good place to stop and get both supplies and information. If that bitch of a girl had been spotted just a few days out of town, maybe she'd still be there.

It was worth a shot. It had to be. He was determined to find her and would not go back to the Master again as a failure.

This time he'd make sure she was dead and stayed dead if he had to cut up her body and burn it as well for good measure. He'd gotten a third chance from the Master he didn't deserve. He knew there wouldn't be a fourth. No one was ever that lucky.

He had no intention of having to make good on his promise to be a test subject. It was him or the girl, and it damn sure wasn't going to be him.

He walked along in a huff, dodging low-hanging branches and weaving through a maze of underbrush as quick as he was able.

There was a road, but he wasn't about to take it. Not

when he could skulk about in the woods. The forest would give him better protection should he happen upon anyone, even if they were a pain to navigate.

Lucien dodged another root and almost ran into a low-hanging vine in the process. He swore under his breath. These distractions weren't doing him any good. No matter, he'd be through the woods and in Stratton soon enough.

He rubbed his jaw with one hand and got back to walking. It still hurt from where the Master had grabbed him, as did his shoulder. He brought his hand away and saw fresh blood on it. The sight of it angered him.

How dare the Master treat him like a common swine! He was so much greater than the other bandit what's-his-name with the one eye and the scarred face. How could the interloper get the credit and he gets cast aside like a toddler? It wasn't fair, and his honor demanded retribution.

Once he was done with this mission and that little slip of a girl was in the ground, he'd find freak show face and cut him open as well. Put the poor sop out of his misery as recompense for the slight. No one should ever see him grovel and live.

It was partially his own fault. If he'd succeeded in his mission in the first place, none of this would have happened. That didn't matter to him, not now. He was too angry to be rational.

He ran forward another few steps and tripped on another root, tumbled over, and landed face first in the dirt.

The ground was wet from a recent rainstorm and his face was now covered in both blood and mud. A fine sight for anyone to see. Not that anyone ever would, he'd see to that, but it was the principle of the thing.

Even nature itself seemed to be out to get him. He'd see nature pay, too, if needed. He knew little of nature magic, but he was so mad he swore he'd learn it later and come back to twist the tree that slighted him.

As he got up and wiped the mud off his eyes and chin, he heard the sound of laughter off in the distance. The sounds were coming from the west.

Instantly, he froze. Then, he darted his eyes around to make sure he was still well hidden. Satisfied, he crept forward to get a closer view of the travelers. He had no idea who these cheery interlopers were, but they would be the first to face his full fury.

Harvey laughed out loud and punched Gabriel in the arm. "Good one, Gabe," he said. "I'd never heard that joke before."

Gabe smiled back at the kid and laughed as well. "I thought so, too."

"Where'd you hear it?"

"Well, I heard it years ago at this seedy bar in a little town called-" Gabe stopped talking as he noticed Sariah wasn't joining in on the fun. "What's wrong, Sariah? Didn't get the joke?"

She gave him a smug smile. "Oh, I got it all right. I just didn't find it all that funny."

Gabe and Harvey stopped and turned to face her. "Why not?" Harvey asked.

Sariah put her hands on her hips and shot him an icy glare. "What's so funny about a woman on the floor with her knickers up over her face, anyway?"

Harvey grimaced. "Uh, nothing, I guess?"

"Humph. Men." She turned away from them. In the same instant, Bear barked at the two men disapprovingly and turned as well.

Harvey put a hand on her shoulder and turned her to face him. "Come now, I'm sorry. Neither of us meant any harm by it."

Sariah gave him a deadpan expression, then she broke into laughter. "Just kidding," she said through raucous laughter. "It was funny as hell. You should have seen your face, though!"

Harvey gave her a pouting look, but then he and Gabe joined her and they all laughed together for a few minutes before continuing.

"So how much further away is this complex supposed to be?" Harvey asked Sariah as they got moving again.

"Not much further, if my source was telling the truth. It's supposed to be buried under a ruin of the old world. Couldn't miss it, they said."

"How much faith can we put into this source of yours?" Gabriel asked. "Remember, I don't even know where this place is supposed to be, and I used to be one of them."

Sariah stood firm. "I trust her. That should be good enough for you, too."

Gabe grumbled but relented. "Ugh. Fine."

They started walking forward once more, not noticing that behind them, Bear began to growl.

Lucien blinked twice to be sure. He couldn't believe his eyes. Were the Bitch and the Bastard finally being nice to him? Were things finally going in his favor? He had to be sure.

He cast his invisibility spell and crept out of the woods toward the group. It didn't take long, maybe twelve steps out into the open before he was certain.

There before him, walking, was his quarry, and not just the girl, but most of her crew as well. The short dwarfish guy with the big axe wasn't there, but the two tall guys were.

Maybe the big fat oaf had gotten killed in the fire. Sacrificed himself to get the others to safety or some such.

Regardless, it was them, all right. They were right in front of him, heading his way. Best of all, they had no idea he was there. He had the element of surprise on his side at last!

He took out a pair of daggers and clenched his jaw, which made it start hurting again. He liked the pain. It would serve him well as he carved the flesh off all of their bones one by one.

Lucien took another few steps and that's when he saw it. The mangy mutt was with them again. Mental magic wouldn't work on the stupid beast. He'd need a different plan.

Thinking fast, he decided to lure the animal into the forest, and take it out by itself. He could work his spells in peace and get his quarry to run into the forest at the same time. It was genius.

He picked up a small pebble and threw it in the stupid beast's direction. The animal seemed to notice, and his human targets did not.

Lucien smiled.

He threw another pebble. This time, the dog looked in his direction. Lucien waved at the beast brazenly for good measure.

The dog snarled and gave off a low growl, then started coming his way.

Lucien's smile got bigger. Everything was going to plan.

Bear shot forward toward the trees faster than Sariah had ever seen him move before. The dog was barking like mad and rushing like he was going into battle.

"Wait, Bear!" Sariah called after him, but it was no use. The animal kept going.

"What's gotten into your dog?" Harvey asked Gabe.

The older man shook his head. "I don't know. The only other time I saw him act like this was when you and Sariah were under attack by that massive wolf."

Harvey cocked his head to the side. "You don't suppose there's someone in trouble out there, do you?"

Gabe shrugged. "Don't know. It's possible. Regardless, we don't have time to stop for that sort of thing."

Sariah scowled at him. "Come now! What does it say about us if we can't help out an innocent bystander in trouble? Or at least go after Bear."

He looked toward his dog, who had almost reached the

edge of the woods. "Don't worry, I'm sure Bear will come back soon enough. He knows how to find us."

Sariah scowled at him. "You mean you're not even going to go after him?"

Gabe chuckled. "Remember what happened last time?"

Sariah's frown grew and she shot him an icy glare.

"Yeesh, sorry. No, I'm not going to chase him. Why should I? We're on a mission, remember? We have to stay on track and it's not safe out here."

"But someone could really be in trouble out there. We have to go help!"

Gabe shook his head. "No, we don't. We have to stay on target."

Sariah scoffed and turned to look at Harvey. "I suppose you feel the same way?"

Harvey gave her a glib look and shrugged.

Sariah shook her head and glared at both of them. "Men," she said. She unsheathed the sword at her side. "I guess I'm going to have to do this my way, then."

With that, she ran off after Bear before either of them could stop her.

"Wait!" Gabe and Harvey cried out in unison.

Lucien stopped just inside the woods and caught his breath. That mangy mutt was still following him.

Good, he thought. Things were going in his favor. He would win the day. He rubbed his hands together greedily and waited. Now he just needed for that stupid dog to get close enough.

Lucien crouched onto the ground and his eyes darted around. Where was the damn dog anyway? The beast had been close on his heels not a moment before, and now it seemed to have gone completely quiet.

A moment later, a mass of fur and claws leaped out from under cover of a nearby bush, heading right in his direction. The beast howled as it made a beeline for his throat.

Lucien was ready. He ducked and moved to the side to dodge out of the way of the beast's lunge. The dog ended up missing him by a couple of inches.

He lunged at the dog with one of his daggers, but the stupid beast was quick on his feet and the animal managed to dodge his advance.

Bear lunged at him again and this time he managed to force Lucien to the ground. The two tumbled around in the undergrowth for a moment, both vying for control.

Lucien kneed the animal in the side as hard as he could and managed to get Bear off him, then he scrambled back to his feet.

The mangy mutt bared its teeth and pounced again, but Lucien was ready for him. He rolled to the side and swung out with his good hand in a backhanded swing. His blade connected with one of the dog's paws, injuring the beast at last.

Bear howled in pain and limped backward. He bared his teeth and growled. It looked like he would pounce again.

Lucien looked at the wounded animal and was pleased with himself. With one paw injured, he wouldn't be able to chase him very well, but the thing still had a lot of fight left in him. Too much, in fact. He could keep fighting, but before long Bear's friends would catch up.

That would ruin the rest of the plan.

He couldn't have that. He spat at the creature and ran away into the woods. Fortunately, the dog didn't follow this time. Regardless, phase two of his attack was now beginning.

This was bad. Sariah was off somewhere in the woods by herself and there was something else out there with her. What it was, Gabe wasn't certain. He reached out with his magic but couldn't sense anyone in the immediate vicinity.

Worse, Bear lay at his feet, wounded. The dog would most likely be fine with a good bandage and a week or two of rest, of course, but that wasn't the bad part. He inspected the wound again.

There was no mistaking it. The wound was from a weapon, not an animal. There was a human out here, one with malicious intent, that was most likely hunting Sariah. The assassin, Gabe thought, would make sense. They were close to a hidden Dusk Raven base.

A knot of fear formed in his gut and he clenched his fists. Whoever it was, they couldn't have gotten very far.

Gabe signaled for Harvey to unsheathe his weapon but do it quietly, while he did the same. The kid complied readily. Then he put his fingers to his lips to signal the kid to be quiet. He nodded and made a similar motion with his own hand.

That made him feel better. He wasn't sure what they'd

find out here in the woods today, but he knew stealth would be needed if they didn't want to end up wounded and on the ground like Bear.

He knelt and put a hand on Bear's head to comfort the dog, then got back up and pointed further into the woods. Harvey seemed to get the message and the two of them left the dog behind and started creeping through the trees.

Gabe felt bad about leaving Bear behind, but if their attacker had let him live, it was because he wasn't going to come back to finish the job. The animal was safe enough, and he needed to conserve his energy for the possible battle ahead.

He thought about casting an invisibility spell over the two of them to hide their movements but thought better of it. With how much noise they were making skulking through the trees, invisibility wouldn't do them a lot of good.

The two made it several more steps before Gabe heard the unmistakable sound of labored breathing from off to his left.

His whole body tensed, and he had to work to calm his nerves. Whoever their quarry was, they were in the small clearing just ahead.

He pointed a finger at Harvey and then pointed with his sword arm off to the left. The kid nodded. He got the message.

Gabe gripped his sword even tighter until his knuckles turned almost white. Then, he charged forward into the clearing with a loud battle cry.

CHAPTER EIGHTEEN

Sariah screamed and shielded her face as someone came crashing through the trees behind her, weapon raised and at the ready. She let her weapon drop as she shrieked and fell to the ground to try and get away from her new opponent.

Gabe and Harvey looked at her crumpled on the ground and almost laughed to ease the tension.

With a huff, she got off the ground and onto one knee. "How could you?" she demanded.

The two men looked at each other.

"Us?" Harvey whined, pointing at his chest and then at hers. "We thought you were the enemy!"

Sariah did a double take. "Me? The enemy? Are you crazy, I thought you were the enemy!"

Harvey extended a hand to help her up the rest of the way, which she readily accepted with a "thank you." She then proceeded to dust herself off.

"Wait a second," Gabe said. "If you thought we were the enemy, why did you crumple to the ground like that?"

Sariah glanced at herself and back at him. "Who me?"

Gabe nodded.

"Well, you made that gods awful racket coming through those trees and scared me half to death! What was I supposed to do?"

Harvey giggled under his breath.

Gabe scoffed. "What happened to your combat training? All those afternoons I spent training you for a real confrontation, where was that?" he asked in an accusatory tone.

Sariah gave him a sheepish grin, then wiped it off her face a moment later. "Look, none of that matters right now."

Gabe gave her a confused look.

"The real enemy is still out there, right? He could be anywhere. While you're standing there accusing me, he could be right on the other side of the trees preparing to pounce."

Gabriel frowned and Harvey looked chastised. Both of them muttered something along the lines of an apology, which Sariah accepted quite gracefully.

The corners of Lucien's lips turned upwards into a big grin.

If only the stupid girl knew just how right she was, he thought as he watched the scene play out in front of him.

There the three buffoons were practically genuflecting in front of each other while their real danger was so close he could smell what they ate for breakfast.

Yes, he thought. Fortune is smiling on me. Soon, I shall get my due.

He tightened his grip on both blades. In the process, he noticed a small gash on his left arm. The stupid dog must have gotten in a good swipe during the earlier struggle.

No matter. His arm felt fine, and he could kill them all with one weapon anyway if need be.

He reinforced his invisibility spell and took a small step forward, then another and another. He was not ten feet away from the three of them now, almost within striking distance. No games this time. No leaving his weapon visible. This was his moment to shine, and he was done playing.

They didn't have a clue.

The hairs on the back of Gabe's neck stood on end. Something was wrong. He sniffed the air. Bear's attacker was there. He was sure of it. He couldn't see him, but he could smell and sense him sitting on the edge of the clearing.

If he was going to turn things around and get the drop on their attacker, he needed to act like he didn't have a clue.

He made a grand gesture of genuflecting in front of Sariah in apology for the earlier slight, all the while keeping one eye toward the edge of the clearing where danger lay hidden.

Sariah and Harvey were mumbling something to each other, but he didn't catch it. He wasn't really listening.

He heard the sound of a tree branch crunching underfoot from behind them and knew he was right. The enemy was there.

He wondered if it was the same assassin who had killed Sariah's parents. He supposed he had no way to know for sure, but it would certainly explain why he couldn't see the man. Invisibility wasn't complicated, but there were still few who used it.

No doubt the killer wanted to complete his mission and kill "the one that got away."

He didn't have long to muse, though, for in that same instant, he heard the faint noise of a twig breaking behind him. The assassin must have finally moved from his place of hiding.

Gabe crouched low to the ground and struck out backward with his blade in the direction of the earlier noise. He heard a metal "clang" as his sword impacted something else metallic and then a grunting noise as his thwarted assailant fell to the ground beside him.

The commotion was enough to rouse both Sariah and Harvey from their joviality and they both readied their weapons.

Gabe looked around for the assailant, but no one was there. It was unnerving trying to fight someone who wasn't there, but he wasn't sure what else to do. He had to protect Sariah.

He made a few broad strokes with his blade in every direction around him. The others did the same, but nothing connected. Not that he expected it to. The assassin was smart and no doubt had reared back to pounce again.

A moment later, another attack came. He heard the sound

of his opponent's movements just in time to deflect most, but not all, of the blow. The killer's dagger made a sickening slicing sound as it ran up the length of his sword arm.

Gabe howled in pain and dropped the blade to the ground. With his other hand he punched in the direction the dagger had come in and managed to contact something hard. He heard a gasp as he knocked the wind out of the killer, then took a step back.

He took a half-second to spare a look at the wound on his arm. It looked nasty but felt superficial. He'd heal it once the battle was over.

Meanwhile, Sariah had crept over to him and placed her back against his own for shared safety, while Harvey was making broad sweeps all over trying to find his opponent the brute force way.

Gabe heard the sound of Sariah swallowing hard. Her heart was beating fast in her chest. She was scared. He had to find a way to end the conflict quickly.

He used his magic to try and force his sword up from the ground and into his hand, but along the way it managed to bump into something invisible. Their attacker grunted again before sprawling on the ground, visible at last.

Sariah gasped as she took in their attacker's face. The sudden noise distracted Gabe just enough that he didn't see Lucien recover and lunge at him.

The killer got a good swipe in at Gabe's middle and he almost doubled over in pain before he punched the man on the side of the head to force him backward.

"You!" Sariah shouted. She threw her sword in Lucien's

direction, but it bounced off his leather tunic and landed harmlessly in the grass.

Lucien stared at her with a rabid hunger in his eyes. He started to get back up again, but Gabe had enough. The older man made a few motions with his hands and conjured a fireball to fling at Lucien.

The assassin squealed when he saw the flames rising and just like that, he disappeared again. Where he went was anyone's guess.

Moments later, the tension left the air and Gabe let the fire in his hands die. Clutching his stomach with his good hand, he slumped over onto the ground.

Lucien scowled. He had expected Sariah's little friends to be handy with a blade, but he hadn't expected a magic-user to be among them.

He thought the Dusk Ravens had magic on lockdown, and yet here he was, having swords fly around and fireballs coming out of nowhere! What the hell?

No matter, he'd wounded the magician pretty well, and suffered only minor injuries to boot. He'd recover. The enemy mage remained to be seen.

The mage wasn't his target though. That stupid girl was and now that her mage protector was down, there was only one guardian left to deal with.

A smile crept across his lips. Unless, he thought, I can lure her off on her own...

He picked up a small stone and waited a moment. The

big oaf knelt next to the mage in the field, but the girl kept looking about.

Perfect.

He made himself visible again for a brief moment and flung the stone at her back. It hit her squarely. She turned and looked straight at him. The two locked eyes for a half-second, then he waved and disappeared.

It was enough. The girl started running in his direction. Now all he needed was another place to sit and wait to ambush her, far away from her friends.

And he knew just the place.

Harvey knelt beside Gabriel. "Are you okay?" he asked the older man.

Gabe chuckled. He looked at the wound in his stomach. "Oh, you know. I've been better, I guess."

Harvey felt the wound. It was deeper than it looked. How deep was hard to say, but Gabe certainly wasn't in good shape. He guessed that without proper care the man had hours to live at best, and there wasn't much by way of quality care all the way out here.

Best to keep him happy for as long as he could, he supposed.

"I'll say," Harvey replied. "That guy really got the drop on you, didn't he?"

Gabe nodded. "I suppose you could say that. He had the advantage, being invisible and all. You're lucky to have someone with you who knows what that's like."

"Huh." Harvey rubbed his chin with one hand. "I guess so. That's quite the trick, you know."

"Do I ever." Gabe coughed and more blood gushed out of the wound. He winced in pain.

Harvey put his hand back over the wound. "Easy, now. You've lost a good amount of blood. Might want to take it slow."

Gabe just nodded.

The younger man got to work quickly, tearing off a piece of his shirt and making a makeshift bandage he used to tie Gabe's wound shut as best he could. It wouldn't do much to stem the blood flow, but it would maybe slow it a little .

"That ought to help some," he said with one of his signature goofy grins.

Gabe smiled weakly at him. "I hope so."

"Can you, you know, heal yourself?"

The older man looked down at his wound. "You know, I've never tried with a wound this size. It's possible, I suppose. It'd take some time, though."

Harvey patted him on the shoulder. "I'll have Sariah get you something to make yourself comfortable so you can focus on it while I build you a fire."

He turned then. "Hey Sariah," he started, but she was nowhere to be found. Once again, she'd run off without them.

No doubt she was running after her parents' killer. Harvey frowned. How could Sariah be so brash? It was irritating to say the least. They'd have to talk about this when things settled down.

He got up to run after her, looked around a couple

times, then sat back down.

"What's wrong?" Gabe asked him.

"Hmm? Oh, Sariah's gone is all."

Gabe laughed and clutched his wound once again. "Well go after her already."

Sariah sprinted as fast as she could. She could see Gabe was hurt and thought about stopping to help him, but she couldn't take the chance of losing her quarry once again. He was out there. She knew that with certainty now.

Besides, Harvey was with Gabe. He wouldn't leave an injured man in the lurch, and Gabe could heal himself with his magic-y stuff.

She bit her lower lip. Maybe she should go back. It's what either of them would have done for her.

Sariah growled and put even more energy into her run. Going back was the right thing to do, but she had started this mission for a reason, and she would see it through to the end. Once she succeeded, she could go back for the others. They'd be safe enough out in the woods, and she could find them again with her mental magic trick.

They would understand. They had to understand. This was her mission. She couldn't let the killer get away again.

Her hunt for the killer wasn't going well. He had gone invisible again, so he could be practically anywhere, and she didn't have a clue where to start looking.

She pouted for a minute then headed east through the trees. He would be heading back to his little base, of course. It was the only move that made sense. He'd want to regroup and recover before attacking again.

That, and let one of his victims bleed out on the ground so there'd be fewer opponents.

Sariah groaned again. She really should go back for Gabe, not that there was much she could do about it if he was going to die anyway, but she felt bad, and the guilt was starting to eat away at her. What kind of victory would it be if it cost the life of a friend?

She heard the sound of someone grunting as they fell to the ground not far off in front of her. It was her parents' killer. There was no one else it could be all the way out here.

With renewed vigor, she shot forward in the direction of the noise, taking great care to make sure she didn't trip and fall like the other guy had. The undergrowth was particularly thick out here.

Lucien almost chuckled, but the noise would have given away his position. Things were going swimmingly. So well, in fact, he'd dropped his invisibility spell for the moment. It was taxing physically to keep it going and he wanted plenty of energy for the task ahead.

With only the dumb bitch after him now, it would be easy enough to take her out.

He smiled as he thought about what he'd do to her corpse and in his excitement managed to trip over another root sticking out of the ground and fall over. He grunted as he fell.

Lucien swore and dusted himself off, then got back up. He chided himself for his overconfidence. He'd have to be more careful. It wasn't much farther now.

The woods gave way to the ruins, and the girl was still fast on his heels. She was following him with almost unnatural ability. He wondered about that for a second, then let it drop. It didn't matter how she followed him, only that she did.

Giant hunks of stone and glass jutted out of the ground. Before him lay the ruins of an old, stone tower still partially standing. He was here. The place where the final showdown would take place. Just up ahead was an alcove where he would wait for her.

His lips twitched with anticipation. He would be victorious at last.

Sariah stopped for a second to catch her breath.

She was standing amidst a group of giant structures made out of stone, glass, and some sort of twisted metal that seemed to grow out of the underbrush like twisted, man-made trees. It was surreal to look at.

Could this be the ruin Valerie had told her about? It had to be.

Sariah started moving more cautiously. Her opponent could be anywhere in this tangled mess, and she'd have no way to know for sure. She needed a plan, but what?

A thought came to her then, unbidden. Her attacker was invisible, sure, but magic could find things you couldn't see, like how she'd found Harvey even though he was far away from her. Magic could help her locate her parents' killer, too.

It was a long shot, but it was the only chance she had right now. Now that she'd seen him in the flesh, really seen him, it might just work.

She knelt on the ground and tried to calm herself as best she could, but it was no use. Her heart was beating so hard with anticipation it was roaring in her ears.

She decided to channel that feeling into her thoughts instead. In her mind's eye, she painted a picture of the only thing she could think of at that moment, something she knew with complete clarity, the killer's face.

Harvey ran forward through the trees. He should be more careful, he figured, but he didn't have the time. He had to save Sariah.

She'd run off on him again. It was becoming somewhat of a thing these days, and not one he liked. He needed to find her and save her before the killer got to her, and he had to hurry to do that. He didn't know how much of a head start she had.

He moved as fast as he could, covering the distance in great strides. At one point, he tripped on a bush and fell flat onto the ground, managing to skin his knees and get the wind knocked out of him all in one go.

He didn't let it stop him for long. He knew he didn't have long before Sariah would be too far away for it to matter.

Harvey checked the sun overhead again to make sure he

was heading east. He was going toward the phantom ruin Sariah had spoken so much about over the last three days. If she was headed anywhere, it would be there.

He decided to slow down so he could catch his breath. Then he saw it, a massive jungle of twisted metal, giant stones, and shattered glass. It was like nothing he'd ever seen before.

This must be the ruin he'd heard so much about. Now all he had to do was find Sariah.

An ear-piercing scream broke through the silence. It came from further on in the stone jungle. It was Sariah's voice, and she was in trouble! He took off.

She'd done it. She'd managed to sense the attacker's direction. He was somewhere deep inside the ruins. Where exactly, she wasn't positive, only that if she kept going in the direction she was currently headed, she'd find him.

Sariah gripped her sword tighter. She looked at her knuckles. They were white from the strain, but she wasn't going to get surprised and crumble apart like she had out in the woods. This time, she was going to succeed.

A sickening feeling of fear and being watched came to her, then. It almost felt like she was being hunted, or maybe the one doing the hunting, she couldn't quite tell. It was disorienting.

Sariah slumped down to the ground and clutched her head as vile thoughts of blood and carnage washed over her. These weren't her thoughts, were they?

They couldn't be. They must belong to the killer, to

Lucien. That was his name. She could sense it as clearly as she could sense her own, and so much more about the twisted man.

She remembered then that this particular mental magic trick did more than just tell you where to find them. It also made you almost a part of them, and let you read their thoughts and feel their feelings.

Nausea hit her and she retched as another wave of his awful thoughts washed over her. She almost threw up, but there was nothing in her stomach to vacate. She'd skipped breakfast that morning. How could she have known at the time where the day would head?

She had to remain strong and fight against Lucien's twisted thoughts. She could win if only she could find him.

Slowly, Sariah got up off the ground. She checked her grip on her blade, then started inching forward slowly. Lucien was up ahead, waiting for her in a building just a few feet in front of her. She knew it like she knew her own hand. This was it, the moment she'd been waiting for.

With her teeth clenched against the hideous thoughts, Sariah kept pushing forward. As she went along, she could sense he was waiting in an alcove to the left of the entrance. He would pounce on her once she got close enough.

What he would do to her afterward was something no one should ever think about. He was truly an awful person, this Lucien.

She knew his plan now and could guard against it. She just had to fight against his thoughts a little longer.

Just a few more feet and it would all be over.

Carefully, quietly, like she was completely unaware, she

crept forward a bit more. She didn't dare to even think about what she would do next, in case doing so somehow tipped him off.

The slightest hint of her shoulder crossed into the building in front of her and she gripped her sword tighter.

Lucien's grinning face filled her mind completely. She could sense him tensing, as he got ready to pounce on her.

Then she took a deep breath and screamed as loud and as hard as she could.

The sound startled Lucien and he fell, visible, onto the ground in front of her. She lashed out with her sword toward his fallen form.

Her sword raked against Lucien's back and made a sickening sound as his skin tore open. She felt a tinge of the pain rock through her body and convulsed.

Lucien howled and spun to the side to get away. He scrambled to his feet in front of her.

You little bitch, a voice reverberated in her head. Whether it was Lucien saying it or thinking it was anyone's guess.

The twisted man lunged at her with one of his blades. She was disoriented as she both watched the attack and, at the same time watched him make it through his own eyes.

She put up her sword to deflect the blow but was only partially successful. His dagger managed to slice open one of her fingers.

Sariah winced at the pain and thrust out with her own sword again, but the blade didn't find purchase. The little man was surprisingly agile and quick on his feet, even in his wounded state.

Lucien leaped to the side and came at her again with

both daggers held out in front. He made a wild sweep toward her middle, which she dodged just in time.

That was followed up with an upward swipe toward her chest and neck. One of those swipes connected. She felt a surge of pain flow through her as Lucien's dagger bit into the tender part of her breast.

She spun to the side to get away and thrust out with her sword at the same time. The motion forced Lucien backward, which gave her a moment to stop and catch her breath.

Sariah wasn't sure how, but she had to slow the man down. He was too much for her.

With fury in her eyes, she howled and made a desperate lunge forward, aiming for one of his arms. Her blade connected and made a strange "thunk" noise as it impacted bone.

The assassin howled and dropped the blade in that hand.

Sariah smiled. With only one dagger, he'd be easier to take down. She pulled back on the blade to free it and made a wild swipe for his head but came up empty. The little man dodged out of the way and spun around toward her side.

He made a backward swipe with his dagger that caught her off guard and managed to slice open part of her sword arm.

Sariah winced and dropped the blade. In the same motion she kicked out at Lucien, hoping to force him to the ground. Her boot connected with one of his knees and he fell.

But the assassin was quick-thinking, and he grabbed

and pulled on Sariah's clothes as he tumbled, pulling her down as well.

The two lay on the ground for a moment, then Lucien punched her in the side and managed to come out on top. He put both his hands around her neck and started to squeeze.

Sariah tried to scream but couldn't. The pain was so intense she dropped the mental connection with her assailant, which helped clear her mind but did nothing for her current situation.

She put her hands on Lucien's arms and tried to pull them off her, but it was no use. He was the stronger of the two.

Was this how she was to die?

No, she thought, determined. An idea came to her. Lucien's dagger. She still had it.

With what little strength remained, she reached one hand down toward her side and tried to find the blade's handle. Her vision was starting to get cloudy, and she could feel her life leaving as she rummaged around hopelessly.

Then she had it. She grabbed ahold of the handle and pulled the blade free and shoved upwards as hard as she could.

The blade ripped open a giant hole in Lucien's stomach. The stunned assassin let go of her instantly and fell backward onto the ground, clutching the new wound.

Sariah took a couple deep breaths, then managed to get up on her knees. She looked at her attacker square in the eye. He was hurt badly, but not quite finished.

Lucien looked back at her then, a look of hatred mixed

with longing in his eyes. Sariah saw her own eyes mirrored in them, burning with a similar disdain.

"Please," Lucien said through bated breath. "Please kill me."

Sariah looked at him then not as an enemy combatant, but as a creature to be pitied.

She wondered if she could kill someone in cold blood. She wasn't sure. This Lucien had caused her so much pain, but she'd never killed anyone before, and suddenly, she wasn't sure if she should.

"Please," Lucien repeated. "If you knew what waited for me, you would consider it an act of mercy. You don't know what the Master is capable of. If you did, you'd kill me out of pity. And then you'd run like hell."

The killer slumped over further. She looked at his wounds. They were bleeding profusely. The man likely didn't have long to live. In reality, this was more of a mercy killing.

She didn't need any more urging. The man was evil personified, and she hated him for it. She would do it. She tightened her grip on the dagger and stood fully, then took a half step forward.

With one quick swipe, the deed was done.

Sariah took a couple of breaths to calm herself, then backed away from Lucien's dead body and slumped up against a nearby wall. There, in the safety of the alcove, she cried.

CHAPTER NINETEEN

When Harvey found Sariah, she was sitting and crying. In her hands, she held the assassin's dagger.

The assassin himself was dead a few feet away in a pool of his own blood.

It looked like things were finally over. Sariah's quest had reached its end.

He looked her up and down. She was a little worse for the wear but thankfully appeared to be mostly unharmed.

"Thank goodness you're safe!" he shouted. Sitting next to her he wrapped a big arm around her. She was shaking from the stress and the pain of the day. With his other hand, he wiped a tear from her eyes and pushed back some of the hair that had fallen into her face.

"Shh," he said slowly as they both rocked back and forth.

"It's…it's-" Sariah replied through her sobs.

He put a finger on her lips. "It's over," Harvey finished for her. "I know. I saw. Well, heard, really. I heard you screaming and came running as fast as I could."

"Not the fastest kid, are you?"

Harvey smiled. Normally he was the one to crack the jokes in the hard times, and here she was doing it for him. It made him feel proud.

"Hey, you did great for yourself out there. Looks like you didn't need me anyway." He gently rubbed the base of her chin. "I'm proud of you, you know."

Sariah tilted her head to look at him, a look of confusion in her eyes. "Proud of me? For what?"

Harvey gave her one of his dopey grins. "For finishing this thing. For avenging your parents without getting yourself killed in the process."

She tsked and looked away. "Some achievement."

He took her head in his hand and forced her to look at him. "Hey!" he argued. "I mean it. You were amazing out there. And I got you to stop crying, didn't I?"

Sariah nodded and giggled, then started crying anew.

"It's okay," he offered. "Shh, it's going to be just fine." He hugged her as tight as he could and the two gently rocked back and forth, holding each other and saying nothing for several minutes.

After what felt like hours, Sariah finally stopped crying. To her surprise, Harvey was still sitting next to her, holding on to her like her life depended on it.

She wondered briefly why no Dusk Ravens had come out to investigate the earlier fight. The two of them weren't all that hidden in this tiny spot.

Then, she'd never seen so much of a hint of a doorway

to an actual lair. For all she knew they were still a mile from the entryway. She decided to count herself lucky.

She wiped the tears out of her eyes with the back of her hand and looked at her friend. There was a hint of tears in his own eyes, as well.

There was more there, too. Worry, yes, and caring, but also a hint of longing. She sensed his desire for her.

She didn't know if it was her vulnerability that had finally made his feelings surface or the strangeness of the day and the rawness of their emotions. It was hard to know for sure, only that he wanted her.

And at that moment, she wanted him, too.

"It's crazy how everything worked out, don't you think?" she asked him.

Harvey nodded his big head and smiled at her. It was his signature dopey grin, but it didn't look all that dopey.

Slowly, Harvey started to lean in. She knew what that meant. He aimed to kiss her.

His head kept coming and she turned her own to accept it, but at the last moment, Harvey turned his face away from her.

He backed up and blushed. "Sorry," he muttered under his breath.

"No, it's okay," Sariah insisted. She thought about turning him around and finishing the deed for him, but the moment had passed, and it wasn't coming back.

"So," she started. "Is Gabe okay? He was looking pretty grim back there."

Harvey looked at her and nodded. "He was healing himself when I left him. Swore he'd be fine. That guy is resilient. I wouldn't worry about him."

Sariah smiled. Harvey's cheeks seemed to be returning to their natural color. She supposed that was a good thing. She didn't want him feeling embarrassed.

"And Bear? Tell me Bear is going to make it."

Harvey grinned. "Just a minor wound to one paw. He'll be jumping on you and licking your face again in no time."

Sariah finally relaxed, but just a little. It made her feel better to know her friends were safe, at least for now.

Deep down, she knew the truth. They weren't safe. None of them were. At least, not for long.

Her thoughts went back to the information she'd gleaned when she'd been connected to Lucien's mind. That twisted little man had thought many dark things, but they weren't all about her impending murder.

Some of them had been about other things even more sinister.

Lucien had been after her, true, but not of his own volition. He was but a dagger wielded by someone so much darker. The leader of the Dusk Ravens was her true enemy, a man so shrouded in mystery he didn't have a name and was known only as the Master.

A man so evil, it made Lucien's thoughts pale in comparison.

There wasn't much to go off of, only glimpses of different people and sordid rumors about magical experiments. That and the fact the Master would never, ever, let her or anyone she loved live.

Like it or not, they were all caught up in his mad game now. A game she had no intention of losing.

They were safe enough for today. They could rest and

recuperate from their troubles. It was unlikely word of Lucien's failure would reach the Master's ears too quickly.

When it did, there would be hell to pay and more battles to come, and she was determined to be ready for them.

THE STORY CONTINUES

Sariah killed Lucien, but now The Master wants her dead.

In a race to stop his evil schemes, will anyone survive? Find out in book two, *Betrayal of Magic!*

Grab your copy today at Amazon and Kindle Unlimited

First of all, thank you so much for reading through this entire book, and now for reading through these author notes! It means the world to me to be able to share these characters and this journey with you!

Believe it or not, this is my debut novel! I'd written other books before this one, but this is the first one I've ever actually published, and I'm super excited to be sharing Sariah, Gabe, Harvey, and Bear with the world (especially Bear - I love that mangy mutt).

It's crazy to think that Bear wasn't even in my original outline or idea for the story. When I'd first laid out the plot of the book, no one had any pets! I only added Bear in at the last minute because I felt like Gabe could use a companion all the way out there in the woods. It made his time in the cabin seem way less lonely to me somehow. And since that fateful keystroke, he's fast become one of my all-time favorite characters in the whole series. Hurray for last-minute inclusions!

There were a lot of last-minute inclusions in this book,

in fact. The whole story line took a lot of unexpected twists and turns. See, before I wrote this book, I'd always been a pantser. If you don't know what that is, it's a person that sits down to write with maybe a quick sentence or two in their head and nothing more. Definitely not a full-on outline with a carefully designed plot.

But I had to learn fast. There was an open call for writers to add to the Age of Magic universe and they wanted both a pitch (which I could make in my sleep) and an outline, so I had to hunker down and learn how to plot out not just one book, but an entire four book series all at once, and in a hurry.

The whole thing started shortly after my wife gave birth to our fourth child. I was off of work for about two weeks (let's hope paid paternity leave becomes a thing everywhere soon) and while not taking care of her or watching a mostly sleeping baby, I had a little free time on my hands.

So, one early morning I sat down and wrote the first chapter of this story and roughed out a basic outline for the rest of this book, along with a vague direction for the next three. I did the works – plot summaries for each chapter, character sheets for the Main Characters, rough names for locations, you name it.

I was actually surprised at how fast the whole outline came together, considering I'd never sat down to write with more than a vague idea of where to put the next sentence before, but everything just flowed once I sat down to do it.

Of course, even the best laid plans don't survive contact with the actual writing, so when I sat down to write out said chapters, a lot changed. I guess you can't keep a good panster down, no matter how much you try and domesticate them, eh?

Case in point - originally Harvey never got captured, and Sariah's reasoning for finally deciding to learn magic was . . . not as cool. Let's be glad that happened instead. Also, the final battle with Lucien went down way differently in the outline. It still would have been cool, but this version is still so much better.

So, where does that leave things? What's next for Sariah, Harvey, Gabe, and Bear, you ask? Well you'll just have to read the next book – Betrayal of Magic – to find out. Fortunately, it comes out pretty soon, so you won't have to wait too long.

If you liked this book, *please* leave a review. It means the world to me. Each and every review is like a cherished treasure or a well-loved family heirloom. They're why I write (well that and to get paid, of course, but mostly it's to make readers like you happy). Ever since I was a young boy, I've wanted to share my stories with the world, and I'm over the moon that I'm finally getting that chance.

Plus, a bunch of good reviews *might* just help that next book come out that much faster. There's still loads of adventures for Sariah left in my head just waiting to get put down on paper.

Loved the book a lot? Give me a follow on social media: www.facebook.com/authorpeterglenn OR join my mailing list: www.peterjglenn.com/email. Or heck, do both! The more the merrier!

I'd love to get a shout out from you in either spot and hear about what scene was your favorite, or what you'd like to see in an upcoming Sariah Chronicles adventure. Who knows? Maybe I'll even name a future character after you (if you ask nicely).

Thank you again for joining me on this journey and sticking with it until the very end, and I do hope you'll join with me again in future books.

Auf Wiedersehen.

Thank you for reading our books, sharing with friends and allowing us the opportunity to keep doing what we do.

Telling more stories!

Right now, in my life I am seeking to understand 'the next stage.' For me, the route to becoming an author was five years ago yet seems like another life. I have discussed the highlights of my path so many times, I can't remember any of the indistinct details, only the high points.

I'm not sad about that. I am fully cognizant that I have a limited short-term memory of a lot of things (not all, but many) and prefer to be in the future (where I've created some story I'm in the middle of watching.)

I expect to read my own author notes when I'm in my eighties to remember what happened in my fifties. Hello future me!

Except for the many pictures I assume Peter has of their new child, I can't believe too many parents remember the first couple of weeks. I was so brain-dead from taking care of my little family (and playing video games to combat the stress) that I can't tell you any more than a vague layout of the apartment we lived in at the time.

Oh, and the couch position (but not the couch design) where fresh-from-the-hospital first-born Joshua took a massive leak in the MIDDLE OF THE DIAPER CHANGE. Yes, just imagine a brand-new dad's eyes opening wide when the Yellowstone Geyser shot up mid diaper swap.

It wasn't pretty.

I remember the fear and alarm I felt most.

Bringing out your first book is a lot like that. Fear, and alarm.

Will they like it?

Will anyone even READ it?

Will I get a five-star review?

Will someone troll me and what if they give me a one-star review for a toaster and my book has nothing to do with a toaster and Amazon isn't going to get rid of a wrong review because...

You get the idea, I'm sure. I'm going through my own version of latent-book-release-stress-disorder right now.

Peter, you have accomplished what many aspire to, but few accomplish. The first trip up your mountain of completing a book is (usually) the hardest. Now that you KNOW you can do it, the reality sets in that this joyous and fulfilling career is that.

It is a career.

It's a future which can draw you in, promising sweet nothings in your ear as you feverishly type through the night bringing snippets of your imagination from your brain to the page.

And in the morning, you awake in a daze, wondering

what train hit you last night. You read what you wrote, and a gleam comes to your eye.

You just need to type one more...*just one more line.*

You awake the next morning and start the process all over again.

To you, Peter! May your fevered imaginations bring smiles, tears, and laughter to many readers for decades to come.

Ad Aeternitatem,

Michael Anderle

*Will you be one of the writers to give a new author a review? If you feel up to it, know that it DOES mean so much to authors. We all appreciate your support with our stories but also know that between the two, we would rather you read the fevered imaginations of our brains and grab the next one ;-)

CONNECT WITH THE AUTHORS

Peter Glenn Social

Website: www.peterjglenn.com

Email list: www.peterjglenn.com/email

Facebook:
www.facebook.com/authorpeterglenn

Michael Anderle Social

Website: http://lmbpn.com

Email List: http://lmbpn.com/email/

Facebook:
https://www.facebook.com/LMBPNPublishing